For the McKees and the Spinellis

You can have a hangover from other things than alcohol.
I had one from women.
—Raymond Chandler, *The Big Sleep*

SOUTH SAN FRANCISCO
SEPTEMBER 1997

1

At 4:14 p.m. I was smoking a cigarette. My smoking pattern had finally come full circle. After five religious years of pack-a-day Marlboro Reds, I quit, started up again, switched to Lucky Strike filters, switched to Drum hand-rolling Dutch tobacco, quit, started up on Lucky Strike Straights, switched to American Spirit Blues, quit, started again on American Spirit Yellows, quit, and finally resumed my regimen of Marlboro Reds, a pack a day. I was now convinced that the chemical additives that had driven me to Spirits in the first place would kill me quicker than the cancer the tobacco alone would eventually cause.

By 4:19 the cigarette was burning out in the brown glass ashtray, sending a lone last tendril of smoke in a sacred mission to the ceiling. I looked out the window to the dismal backyard—beaten dirt and broken concrete, straggling stubborn bushes, empty plastic trash bags. I was having a thought, a post-cigarette thought, of fullness, hope, and genuine optimism. It passed quickly. For lack of anything better to do I was reaching for the box of Reds when the phone rang. I looked at it in disbelief and waited a full five rings before I picked it up.

"Hello? Hello? Is anyone there?"

I cleared my throat and remembered I should have spoken first. "Yeah. Crane here."

"Itchy, damn you. Why the hell don'tcha say hello like a normal guy?"

"Whatever gave you the impression I was normal?" It was McCaffrey, a second-rate private investigator down in LA. I had done a local research job for him a couple of years before and never been paid. Since then I'd been fortunate enough to be out when he called. I was looking out the window again, wondering why I had felt so optimistic just a moment before.

"Right as ever, Itchy. Listen, you busy these days?"

I took a moment to shake out another cigarette and toyed with it between my fingers. I didn't have to turn my head to know that my desk was empty, nor did I have to shift my weight to feel the anorexic leather wallet in my back pocket. "Yeah, McCaffrey, I'm pretty busy. Quite a few irons in the fire right about now."

"Well, let 'em get cold. I got one you're gonna want to be in on."

"Fuck you, McCaffrey. Your checks don't bounce, they just never get cut." I hung up.

I lit the cigarette in my hand and leaned my chair back on two legs. I caught a glimpse of myself in the mirror on the far side of the room and realized that my beard was the only part of me not looking thin. I began to have second thoughts about giving McCaffrey the brush-off.

I started my "information services" biz after I walked out of the *San Francisco Chronicle*, drunk off my ass, screaming at the top of my lungs that I didn't want to work with a bunch of fucking drunks anymore. I was right, ironic or not; the alcoholic ratio among journalists looks enough like a whole number to guarantee it will never appear on a racing form. But it was a bullshit reason to quit. I was just tired of endless deadlines writing useless copy that would only end up lining a birdcage. One particularly drowsy afternoon I did the math and worked out how many trees in the dwindling rain forests I was personally responsible for felling and couldn't eat for two days. Besides, the writers for the *Guardian* were getting all the hot stories; I worried I wasn't read by anyone under sixty.

So I moved to South San Francisco and set up shop in a decent little house with two bedrooms upstairs, a spacious living room with bay windows offering nice views of the house across the street, a real kitchen large enough to actually have a kitchen table, and a faux-marble staircase leading to the street. The downstairs was a large garage with an unfinished room in the back. South City is a bedroom community where the pace of life feels slower and more private than in San Francisco proper, and I liked the idea of slowing down and having more time to think. There were few restaurants and fewer bars, and the likelihood that I would stumble into trouble was negligible. This is the kind of place where one moves to raise a family—or, I thought, build a business.

After years of snooping and scooping facts for the paper, I had a pretty good nose. I printed up some business cards and started a PR campaign. I billed myself as a jack-of-all-knowledge, and for a fee would answer any question put to me. I put an ad in the *Guardian*, some friends at the *Chronicle* placed a nice blurb about me in the Sunday edition, and pretty soon I had a nice clientele going. All kinds of gigs: mapping out elaborate travel plans to unusual destinations for people with unusual tastes; sexual fetish information; property ownership inquiries for investors; the occasional person-search for law firms serving subpoenas; even helping students with research projects on obscure subjects. I was like a private dick with very little legwork—and I never got shot at. I even got a couple cushy reconnaissance missions, literally taking some hotshot's vacation for him, all expenses paid, to work out the perfect weekend in Oahu or Cabo so he wouldn't run the risk of staying at a less-than-divine resort. Those were the days.

Then I made the mistake of ghostwriting a cover story in one of the weeklies about nude beaches in the Bay Area. I knew the kid working the story and the money was right. Turns out my directions to one of the harder-to-reach Marin beaches—nude beaches are off the beaten path, even in California—got flubbed somewhere between me, the credited writer of the article, the editor, and the fact-checker. A young couple missed the crucial turn that had been omitted from the printed directions and fell sixty feet to the rocks. Their bloated corpses washed up at low tide and scared the piss out of a couple of Chinese fishermen.

It could have all blown over—should have all blown over—but the girl's mother got word about what the couple were doing out there. She tried, unsuccessfully, to sue the paper, did a lot of grade-A snooping, and made the writer's life hell until he finally confessed that he didn't know the swimming hole but had gotten his information from me. The woman launched a personal vendetta—placed slanderous ads next to mine, got on radio talk shows. I became a headline: "Ghostwriter

Blamed in Young Girl's Death." No one ever asked me for comment. The last two years had been a long, slow slide into insolvency.

I was scraping bottom and I knew it.

My brain was halfway to sending my hand back to the phone to star-69 McCaffrey when the front doorbell rang three times in a row and stopped. I made it to the door in time to see the UPS driver gun his engine and pull his truck away from the curb. I opened the screen to yell at the driver but it caught against something and bounced right back into my face. I took a step back and saw what had impeded me: a flat box, barely four inches thick but six feet high and standing on end, leaning against the outdoor railing.

I muscled the thing downstairs, opened my garage door, and set it up on my workbench. It was addressed to me, overnight delivery, and the return address was missing a name but I recognized it as McCaffrey's Santa Monica digs. I didn't like it. He was playing me, one way or another.

I took a mat knife and ripped into it, cut the top of the box away, and started in on the bubble wrap. When I was all but buried in packing materials I realized I was looking at the backside of a stretched canvas. I stood it up, turned it around with some difficulty, put it up on the bench, and stepped back to light a smoke and have a look.

I never got the smoke lit.

It was a painting of me.

2

"McCaffrey Investigative Agency. Can I help you?" She sounded blond, past her prime, and tragically Los Angeles.

"Give me McCaffrey."

"Mr. McCaffrey is busy at the moment. If you'll leave your name and number I'd be more than happy to—"

"I'm more than happy to talk to him *now*, lady. Tell him it's David Crane on the line."

"I'm sorry, Mr. Crane, but Mr. McCaffrey is quite bus—"

"Miss Moneypenney, tell Mr. McCaffrey that the gentleman on the line is making obscene sexual demands. It won't be a lie if you don't quit talking to me and start talking to him."

There was a short but pregnant pause and the line clicked and my ears were assaulted with an instrumental version of Michael Jackson and Paul McCartney's "The Girl Is Mine." It only lasted about ten seconds.

"Itchy! What's the good word?"

"You tell me. It isn't my birthday, and I don't believe it's the first of April."

"I wanted to be sure that I have your attention, that's all."

"You've got it."

"All right. I could really use your help on this one.

It's a simple missing-person case but I've got nothing to go on. Girl up and bailed. She's of age so the cops won't touch it. Everyone seems to think she just doesn't want to be found—no foul play, no intrigue. But her family is desperate and the money is right."

"That's all very interesting." I let it lie just a moment until I heard him take a breath to speak. "But why do I have a portrait of myself sitting in my garage?"

"So I *do* have your attention." He laughed a small, threatened laugh that I wished I could have beaten out of him. "That's why I called you, Itchy. I figured you wouldn't be able to pass this one up. You're too damn vain."

"Tell me something useful."

"Itchy, I don't know anything more. This is one of the paintings the girl did before she disappeared. The family gave it to me as a possible lead. I thought it looked an awful lot like you, so I sent it along. Thought you might know her. Do you?"

"Well, let's see . . . do I know a girl—no name, no face, no description—who paints portraits of me?"

"Hey, either you sat for the picture or you didn't. You must have, it's too good otherwise."

"She could have done it from a photograph."

"If you didn't sit for it then you know everything I do. The family wants to remain anonymous, so I don't even know the girl's last name. She's probably traveling under an alias anyway. Apparently she hasn't used her real name since she was in kindergarten. All I have is a first name and a little background information."

"What's the name?"

McCaffrey took a sip of something; I heard what sounded like a shot glass clink against the receiver.

"Ashley. The name's Ashley."

My first thought when I put the phone down was that there was a lot I didn't like about the situation. No last name. McCaffrey's cagey drink. The painting. Then I realized that there wasn't anything I *did* like about it. McCaffrey had agreed to have his assistant fax over everything he had on the case and ended the conversation abruptly, making some excuse about a deadline he had to meet. Probably a happy hour.

I thought about having a drink myself. I had finally gotten over Alcoholics Anonymous, a habit almost as hard to kick as the bottle itself, and had simmered down into a quiet, occasional drinker. I cut off all my old drinking buddies when I first got sober, none of my cronies from AA would speak to me after I started drinking again, and the old drunk crew certainly didn't know that I had jumped off the wagon running. But between a bunch of guys in a church basement drinking bad coffee from Styrofoam cups and a group of career drunks facedown on a barroom floor in a pool of whiskey-flavored vomit—a man can do worse than to shake them all.

I went to the vanity in my closet and reached for the musty bottle of Old Crow, got a glass from the kitchen, and poured myself two thin fingers. I took my shot down to the garage, pulled a dusty folding beach chair off the wall, and sat down facing the painting.

I was pictured sitting in a chair in my kitchen, a barber's blouse draped over me with hair all down the front. I had an intense, boggled look on my face. Standing directly behind me, peering down with clippers in hand, was the barber; I recognized him too. He was an old Italian barber from the neighborhood who'd been cutting my hair since I moved to South City, and he made house calls. He looked as elegant and charming as I knew him to be, a glint in his eye illustrated by a skillful touch of the brush. In the background I could see the clutter of my bachelor's kitchen—unwashed dishes, cupboards in bad need of a paint job. The image was exceptional, exquisitely detailed in the folds of the barber's blouse over me, the clumps of freshly shorn hair that fell onto the floor, the gentle illusion of the buzzing of the clippers in the barber's hand, the subtle touch of intention, as if he really were about to lean in and touch up beneath the ears.

Maybe it didn't look *exactly* like me—it wasn't photo-realism, but it wasn't abstract expressionism, either. It looked like me. It was evocative of me. Fuck, it *was* me. Anyone who so much as knew me from high school would get a creepy recognition vibe coming off this painting.

I downed the shot. What was most disturbing was the fact that it seemed to be a scene from my life. The barber was a dead ringer for my barber, who had just given me a trim a few weeks before, and the shirt I was wearing in the picture—the collar visible under the blouse—was a recent acquisition.

Casually, without meaning to do so, my eye wandered down to the bottom edge of the painting. Written clearly in the corner in black, over the dingy yellow of my kitchen tiling: 8/18/97.

I nearly coughed up my drink.

I checked the fax machine and saw the three slim pages

passing for McCaffrey's background information. It was nothing. One page was a photocopy of a California driver's license with all the pertinent information—last name, address—blacked out. The photo was so blurry and distorted from being photocopied and faxed that it told me nothing at all. Ashley _____, five foot two, black hair, blue eyes. No help.

The second page was a form from McCaffrey's agency, a kind of catch-all client information page, also left mostly blank. It told me that Ashley was born somewhere in Los Angeles County in 1976, had grown up primarily in Anaheim, and in her late teens had moved to San Francisco with her mother. Last known address: *Unknown*.

The third page was a copy of a check from the McCaffrey Agency, made out to me, to the sum of $25,000. The memo at the bottom said simply, *Advance on services and expenses*. It was a goose chase, but a well-paid one. I hadn't seen that much money since—well, maybe never.

I reluctantly turned on my ancient Power Mac and got online. This always gave me a twinge of guilt. Were it not for the accursed Internet, and its recent rise in popularity, I might still have a steady income. At first the older, wealthier portion of the population shied away from the Internet, and as they represented the mainstay of my clientele, I managed to hold on to my niche. But as the baby boomers became Internet-savvy, my income dropped off as steadily as Yahoo! stock rose. The bottom line is that the information superhighway made the renegade job title *Information Broker* completely obsolete— almost any piece of information I could obtain could be easily found with a cheap PC, a 14k modem, and a keyword on AOL.

I started with a simple word search on *Ashley* and was bombarded with hits. It would take me a decade to comb through them all, and without knowing anything else about my subject, I wouldn't recognize the right one if I found her. I went to the Social Security site and learned the truly devastating news: from 1983 to 1995, Ashley had been one of the top four most popular baby names for girls in America—top two since '85. Most of them were too young to drive, but there were enough Ashleys in California that I could never hope to wade through them all.

I was cursing McCaffrey's name when he called again.

"Itchy, what's the good word?"

"There are no good words, McCaffrey, you've given me exactly dick."

"Hey, I know it's loose, but if anyone can make somethin' out of nothin', it's you, right?"

I grunted and reached for a cigarette.

"You did get my fax, yeah?"

"Yeah," I said, exhaling a fountain of smoke, "I got it."

"I know you could use the money."

"McCaffrey, I can't cash a fax."

"I know . . . I FedExed you the check, you'll get it in the morning. I just wanted you to see the kind of money we're talking about. If you can find the girl, you'll get that much again."

"You wanna tell me why this girl is worth fifty grand?"

"I'm telling you everything I know. I'll tell you anything I hear when I hear it."

"And the check's in the mail, right?"

"Itchy, if you don't see that check in the morning you call me, all right?"

"Yeah, yeah."

"I gotta motor. Keep me posted."

He hung up. I gave up, turned off the computer, and went downstairs to pull my car out of the garage.

Delores, a 1965 Mercury Comet Caliente convertible, carnival red, 289 v8, four-on-the-floor Hurst shifter, Holley quad-barrel carburetor. I got her for less than three grand back when I was working at the *Chronicle*. I dropped a lot of dough into her and spent many an hour flat on my back underneath her or leaning over the engine with grease under my nails. While she might not be a neck-breaker, I'd pitch her against any car out there for sheer cool cruisability. Old cars are a dime a dozen in the Bay Area, but mine always catches glances.

It's possible to live in San Francisco without a car, surviving on the BART and the Muni and the buses, making it a rare city in America. But the lure of California is predicated on the mythology of the Old West—a horse for every man, the freedom to wander—and owning a car became essential when I moved down to the peninsula. Being freed from the forty-nine-square-mile bubble that is the City of San Francisco opens one up to the full pantheon of locales that make up the larger Bay Area, from Sausalito to San Rafael, from Oakland to Walnut Creek, from Daly City to Redwood City, and all the way down to San Jose.

I always keep my top down, so I hopped in, rolled out of the garage, and took a deep eucalyptus whiff of the red flowering gum trees that line the sidewalk on my street. I drifted down to Magnolia and onto Grand toward the 101 and seated myself at the All Star Café and wolfed a burger with some overdone fries. I thought I'd take a drive down 280 to Pacifica, but as soon as I got onto Old Mission I was done for, and pulled into Molloy's. I parked Delores around back—that .08 blood-alcohol level in Cali scares the hell out of me, and I fully intended on blowing it. I sucked down half a dozen Jamesons, thinking about some twenty-one-year-old babe named Ashley, and before I knew it I was in the back of a cab, nodding off on the way back to Palm Ave., stumbling into my house, and still sitting up at four in the morning, Saturday drunk but feeling sober as Tuesday, staring confusedly into my own reflection on canvas.

3

I woke up late and groggy, shaved my tongue, and tried to wash the taste out of my mouth—like I'd been chewing on an old boot. I showered and cooked a hangover breakfast of hash browns and eggs, sat and smoked sixteen cigarettes, called a cab, and barreled out the door. There was one lead to follow, and I figured I'd better chase it quick.

For the second time in two days I almost killed myself walking out the front door. A flat Fed Ex envelope fumbled its way between my legs and almost sent me sprawling over the rail. I caught my balance, scooped it up, and ripped the zip. Inside was an envelope with my name on it and, sure enough, a check made out to me for $25,000. I almost jumped over the rail voluntarily, but remembered who it was from and doubted it would actually clear.

The cab took me to Molloy's to pick up Delores. I drove straight to the bank to deposit the check, and on my way home I picked up the *Chronicle*, the *Observer*, and the *SF Weekly*. I sat at my kitchen table with a highlighter and a notepad, making a list of every gallery in town that might conceivably hang works by unknowns, with a special eye out for any group shows. I started pounding numbers.

It was slow going. It took me half a dozen calls just

to get over feeling like an idiot: "Hello, are you currently exhibiting anyone by the name of Ashley?"

"Ashley who?"

To avoid answering that question, I settled on playing a dumb college student who knew that a girl from his class had a show but couldn't remember which gallery.

Then I hit pay dirt.

"Dalton Gallery, can I help you?"

"I was wondering if Ashley is part of your group show."

There was a pause on the line. He didn't ask, *Ashley who?* He was quiet for a moment, breathing through his nose. Then, slowly, like a pot of milk coming to a boil and escalating quickly: "Yes, we do have one of her pieces."

"Great. How late are you open today?"

"Four o'clock."

"Thanks."

It was still early, and it was Wednesday, and I usually go to the range on Wednesdays. I figured I had the time and that it would do me good. I didn't feel like having to clean my gun later, so I hopped into Delores and rolled down Grand to the 101 access road and pulled into the Jackson Arms. There was a chill in the air, and the characteristic South City morning fog was stubbornly hanging onto the hills.

"Hey, Charlie, how are you?" Charlie, six foot two, had to be close to two bills, with red-cherry cheekbones, long, stringy hair, and a genuine smile that held one broken incisor. A big gun-toting California redneck, Charlie was salt of the earth and all woman.

"Crane, where you been?"

"Oh you know, here, there."

"Just not here."

"It's been a long week." I was eyeballing the excellent selection of handguns under the glass.

"Got to stay in practice," Charlie said. "Get sloppy, I'll have to show you how it's done—and you don't want to get outshot by a woman."

"I wouldn't mind," I said, "I'm a feminist."

"Pshh," Charlie half-laughed, half-snorted. "You know what I always say: show me a feminist," a wry crooked grin pulled up one half of her face, "and I'll kick her ass."

I'd been eyeballing Charlie's Beretta Cougars. They'd only been on the market a few years and I'd yet to try one.

"You didn't bring your .45?"

"No," I said, "thought I'd take something for a spin." Then I spotted the Mini Cougar .45, so compact and snug, with a pushed-in muzzle—like the pug of automatic pistols, but still packing a mean punch. "Let me try that."

"The Mini Cougar?" Charlie made a face. "It's been sticking. I oiled it yesterday and it didn't help—I gotta break it down. Hey," she moved to another case and reached in, "I know how you love your .45s, man after my own heart and all. But you want to try something with a small profile . . . you ever shoot one of these?" She held up a sleek black snub-nosed automatic, the line between the slide and the frame like a racing stripe. "Gangbanger special?"

"I think you know I haven't."

"First time for everything."

California has a law against renting guns to a single shooter at a range; if you want to rent a gun, you have to bring a friend. This is in response to suicides on shooting ranges, but Charlie has known me for years and always lets it go. "This is the Glock 26, 9mm. The 'Baby Glock.' One of their latest models. Just came out in '96." She loaded up a clip for me, handed me a box of shells, eye protection, ear protection, and a couple of classic red-on-black human silhouette targets. I geared up and stepped into the range, clipped a target onto the rack, sent it out about halfway, and squeezed off the full clip in a single breath. Polymer frame . . . it's a lightweight gun. Easy to imagine why the gangbangers like it. I brought the target back in; it was a nice grouping, right around the heart, with two holes in the middle of the head. I missed one.

I fired off the rest of the box of shells, trying to focus my intention and concentrate on the one thing, the shot, all the while knowing that I was squeezing off my hatred for McCaffrey and my frustration at having to take this bizarre case. The smell of the popping shells helped a little.

"Whattaya think?" Charlie asked.

"A little light for me. Too much like a toy."

I hopped back into Delores and hit the 101 at a trot, driving out of the fog, warming up as I jumped onto 280 and rode it to the end, veering around the sharp bank of the last lonely stretch of freeway with the bay on my right and the City unseen, finally coming up over the steep rise of the exit ramp with the City splayed out ahead of me, the Transamerica winking in the sunlight. The ramp took me over the CalTrain tracks where the trains slow into the depot, down into the depths of the industrial backstreets this side of 80. I went up 6th into SoMa and turned right onto Mission. I was lucky enough to find a parking space right down the street from the gallery, after going around the block only twice. I paralleled and fed the meter.

I stepped into the air-conditioned gallery and saw a cute brunette, early twenties, at the reception desk, talking to a thin-lipped blond man standing at the door to an adjacent office.

"I'll be back in five minutes, I promise," she was saying.

"Go ahead, Serena."

"Thanks, Mr. Dalton." With that, the girl, all trim thighs in a tight skirt, skipped past me without a glance and out the front door.

"Excuse me," I said, stopping Dalton's progress into his office, "are you the man I spoke with on the phone? About Ashley?"

His lips grew even thinner and he inhaled quickly through his nose, stepping around me without looking at me. "You'll find Ashley's piece in the gallery."

I perched at the doorway. "I was wondering if I could chat with you just a moment." I handed him my card. He flipped it over in his wiry hands to see if there was anything on the back before he bothered to read the front. "Information broker? What are you, some kind of investigator?"

"Not really," I forced a laugh, "I'm just doing some research for a journalist who's working on a story about Ashley." I didn't want to spook him. "What can you tell me about the artist?"

He waved me in. His office was immaculate. The desk had one of those month-per-page calendars with appointments lettered in exquisite print, and a telephone that looked as if it had never been touched. The walls were covered with prints of a certain taste: Matisse, van Gogh, Monet.

He sat stiffly behind his desk and blinked at me. He did almost a double take, like he either knew me or was sizing me up for a new sports jacket. "What is it you want to know?"

"Anything, really. But more about her personally. We think her work speaks for itself." I took out a notebook and put a pen behind my ear to look professional. "What is her last name, by the way?"

"I'm sure I don't know," he said, bored. "She's a one-name diva."

"Have you met her?"

"Once or twice," he replied dismissively. "It was quite enough."

"How so?"

"She flounced in here demanding more for her work than I could possibly sell it for—portraits, you know. They just don't go for much these days."

The word *portraits* ran down the back of my neck like stray hairs in a shirt collar after a haircut.

He went on, sighing heavily, casting his eyes at the ceiling: "She wanted to negotiate the gallery's cut, which is *non*negotiable. All lip gloss and no business sense. She's . . . an artist." He smiled, the way one smiles at a crazy cat lady.

The ensuing silence threatened to strangle me. He offered nothing else. Apparently, he was done. "Do you know how we could contact her? An interview would be fantastic."

"Unfortunately, I don't. She acts as her own agent, and when I tried to contact her regarding her share of the sale, her number was disconnected. I'm at a bit of a loss myself."

"The sale?"

"The piece she has in the current show. I sold it."

"To whom?"

He smiled crisply. "That's confidential, I'm afraid. The painting will be collected when the show comes down at the end of the month."

"I see. But you said you met her—what can you tell me about her personally?"

He stiffened visibly, his eyes focused over my shoulder. I turned to see a slick-looking young man, not too tall, but brick-like, standing in the doorway. He wore a silver-gray sharkskin suit, many years out of fashion and very much out of place—but since this was the art world, maybe he fit right in. His loafers were tasseled and shined to perfection. He noticed me staring at him and furrowed a pair of stiff, surly looking brows. Dark hair, deep-set eyes, broad nose. I couldn't place his heritage—not quite Caucasian, but not exactly dark-skinned either. Maybe half-Mexican, or Spanish, or even Italian. His demeanor suddenly relaxed and his lips parted, baring a wide smile generous of teeth but not of intention.

"Oh," he showed us his palms by way of apology, "I didn't realize you had a visitor, Mr. Dalton. So sorry to interrupt." He had a slight accent, a little too much attention on the *h*'s and *r*'s. Definitely a Spanish speaker.

"No—no, not at all," Dalton replied hurriedly. "We're finished. If you'll excuse me—"

"Just one last thing, Mr. Dalton. About that number you said was disconnected, could I trouble you—"

"I'm sorry, Mr. Crane, this gentleman has an appointment." He was done with me. "If you'd like to take a look at the piece, I'll speak with you again shortly."

"Certainly." I stood up and looked down on Sharkskin's snarling brow. He was shorter than me, but not by much, and stocky, with a dangerous, cat-killer look in his eyes. He didn't make a motion to get out of my way, and I couldn't get out the door without knocking him over. "Excuse me," I said, as sardonically as possible.

"Mmmmm," he purred, giving me a coquettish look that was disarming from such a brusque man, and moved aside just enough to let me pass. The second I was out the door it shut behind me.

I cut down the passageway to the gallery proper, the air-conditioning hitting me like a wall of frozen air and drowning out the stagnant silence.

A bright painting fairly illuminated one end of the hall. It was me, wearing fading blue denim Levi's, a gray T-shirt, and a tattered green Mr. Rogers cardigan with six missing buttons and four big holes. That's my sweater, all right. I was bent over my kitchen table, addressing a large envelope, with two more small untidy piles of mail and paperwork on either side of me. The painting had a cool cerulean feel to it, with sharp accents of bright orange in the hair and translucent lime greens highlighting the sweater. Behind my head was a view out the window, barely revealing telephone lines dotted with blackbirds, subdividing a bright, hazy sky, the slight fog reflecting light into the room. My face was bright on one side with the other in shadow, an expression of scattered and nervous concentration on my face. My hand was tense, holding a teal pen with *Bayshore Metals* written on the side. I did some work for a welder at Bayshore and had a ton of their pens floating around my house. The bottom right corner was dated *1/1/96*.

The air conditioner rattled, a yo-yoing, pinging sound from deep in the building, as a similar noise went off inside me.

New Year's Day, last year. I remembered that night. I'd been working on a big project for a historical fiction novelist and was past deadline; the writer wanted everything before Christmas. I didn't go out on New Year's Eve, spent the whole night in my house cranking away, and was rushing to get the package put together and ready to mail first thing in the morning. I remember how stupid I felt when I realized that the post office is closed on New Year's Day.

This was another fucking snapshot of my life.

I had to find that girl Ashley.

I hoped Dalton was done with Sharkskin and I could at least get that number off him and see what kind of damage I could do with it. I still had some pretty good connections at Pac Bell and didn't want to walk out with nothing.

I was surprised to see that Serena still wasn't back, but the door to Dalton's office was slightly ajar. I gave it a hard knuckle rap, just in case.

No response.

"Mr. Dalton?" Still nothing. I gave the door a kick

with my foot and it swung open partway; I ducked my head in and found the office empty. "Mr. Dalton?" I pushed the door the rest of the way and stepped in. There was a faint scent lingering in the air, and I rubbed my fingers together and took a whiff, realizing that I was only smelling a trace of the gun range on my hand. Then I looked over the desk and I wasn't so sure. I could see what looked like the top of Dalton's blond head.

I took another step forward and there he was, tipped back behind the desk, his feet hung up on the edge of his overturned chair, his arms akimbo, and his head askew in a pool of crimson blood. There was a very neat hole right between his eyes, surrounded by a dark, discoloring flash of powder burn. That sound I'd heard wasn't the air conditioner—it was a pistol fired with a supressor.

My heart was in my throat and my feet were out of the office before my brain knew what hit it. It was only the second dead body I'd ever seen, and Dalton with a bullet in his brain was a far cry from my grandmother laid out in a casket embalmed and waiting for the embrace of the worms. I choked my breakfast back where it belonged and stood there a moment in front of Serena's empty area, my thoughts racing.

Ashley, missing; Dalton knew something; fifty thousand dollars. Bells went off. Fifty thousand dollars wants this girl found. That's a lot of dough, even in today's dot-com roller coaster. That's got to be the tip of the iceberg—McCaffrey would never cut me a square deal.

Every two-bit gumshoe from every dime-store novel I'd ever read was jaywalking through my mind. My next thought—to call the cops—was crushed underfoot like a cigarette burned down to the filter and tasting of fiberglass. *Get out, Crane, just get out.* Red exit sign—back of the gallery.

I hotfooted it and found the exit and the typical *Do not open—alarm will sound* notice. I kicked the bar across the door. No alarm. Fuck it, that's retrofitting for you, they can't remember everything. Bright afternoon light, a short trash-can alley. I jumped the chain-link fence and found myself on Minna, and walked calmly around the block to Delores. I found the 101 as quick as I could and headed south.

4

I always did my best thinking driving across the causeway at Brisbane. I would look to my left, feel the wind across my face, and imagine that the South Bay was mine. It was refreshing, the city grit and dirt blowing out of my hair, the bay glorious and blue with white peaks, safe passage to my little chunk of sanity.

None of it added up. Some ditzy twenty-one-year-old artist chick disappears and is suddenly worth fifty grand. McCaffrey hires me—a guy who hates him. The girl likes to paint me, yet I've never sat for a portrait. I get lucky and find her in an art show. Thin-lipped gallery owner knows nothing—or isn't talking—and five minutes later gets dead. No doubt Sharkskin did it, but who the hell was he? And why would anyone want harmless old Dalton dead?

Then the big question hit me: why didn't Sharkskin clip me?

Hold on, Crane, this is reality and you're no shamus. Get a grip and quit thinking like any of this has anything to do with you. Wrong place, wrong time. Lucky you got out before the cops started sniffing.

When I came in the phone was already ringing. I let it ring, thinking the voice mail would get it, before I remembered that I discontinued that service. The phone was still ringing, ten rings and counting; had to be Mc-Caffrey. Better play this one like a private dick—close to the vest.

"Hello?"

"Itchy! Glad I caught ya!" McCaffrey, of course, doing his faux-cheery bit.

"Just getting in."

"I don't have another number for you, Itchy. You still don't have a cell phone?"

"Never needed one."

"Well, I didn't hear from you this morning. Does that mean you got my check?"

"Yeah, I got it. Hasn't cleared yet, though. Jury's still out on you."

"It'll clear, it'll clear. So, how's it going up there? You all right?"

He sounded fishy, fishier than usual. "Yeah, it's all right."

Pause the size of Yosemite.

"Find out anything so far?"

"Nothing to speak of. You got anything else for me or what?"

"Wish I did, pal."

"Well, as much as I'd love to chat with you, McCaffrey, I have an assignment to work on."

I hung up on him. Then I poured myself a drink. Dead bodies and all, seemed like the right thing to do.

I flipped idly through my mail as I sipped. Unpaid bills, disconnection notices, the usual drivel. Then, a robin's egg–blue envelope, lettered evenly bottom to top: *Don't open this in your house.* It was written over and over again, forming a pattern, the words disappearing when seen from arm's length, my printed name and address clearly legible over the top. It was addressed to me in even, simple, slightly effeminate cursive handwriting, no girlie curlicues or rounded dots, postmarked from San Francisco two days earlier. I took a stiff pull of my drink. The whole racket was beginning to give me the creeps.

I put on a sweater, grabbed a fresh pack of cigarettes and the blue letter. I walked up my street and around the corner and up to Sign Hill Park. If you've ever driven from SFO International Airport to San Francisco proper, you've seen the big hill off the 101 emblazoned with the words, SOUTH SAN FRANCISCO, THE INDUSTRIAL CITY. It's a block from my house, and kids go up with flattened cardboard boxes and slide down the letters—the hill is steep, and the letters are sixty feet high. South San Francisco was incorporated in 1908, and even the town's name reflected the industrial plans of its founders. G.G. Swift, who had picked out the territory for stockyards and a cattle market, wanted the site's name to parallel that of his Western Meat Company's plants in South Chicago and South Omaha. Bethlehem Steel and Fuller Paint came to South San Francisco, and the two world wars brought a hefty, if short-lived shipbuilding industry. The sign is now, like many great landmarks, a bit of an anachronism.

I went over to the I in Industrial and copped a squat. The lights of the airport were visible off in the distance, as were the blinking beacons from planes coming in for a landing as a slow fog crept in from Half Moon Bay. I shook my head, called myself a fool, and took the crinkled blue envelope out of my pocket.

I slit it open with a finger and took out a single page and unfolded it. Same handwriting.

David:
   Somehow I fell in love with you. Your phone is tapped.
Be careful. Don't tell anyone about this letter—burn it.
Love,
Ashley.

I cursed myself, calling the entire affair a fat load of hokum even as I took out my Zippo and lit the page, holding the envelope to the flame and letting it catch, holding it up against the view of the bay and the airport and the speeding red tracers of the 101, thinking, *Ashley, my ass.* My fingers got singed and I dropped the ashes and stomped it all out on the I.

Ashley's in love with me? This crazy girl that I've never met? The girl who's gone missing and McCaffrey hired me to find? The girl who's—somehow, someway—painting me? My phones are tapped? Am I supposed to take any of this seriously? Is she in some kind of trouble? And the hell with her, am I in some kind of trouble? What the hell did McCaffrey get me into? And what does any of this have to do with me?

I walked down to the Schoolhouse Deli and bought a fifth of Old Crow. One way or another I was going to need it.

5

It must have been about three in the morning, as I was sleeping the joyous, dreamless sleep of the bourbon drunk, when I heard the three beeps. I once had an alarm system in my house, but the alarm company doesn't come and rip it out when you can't pay the bill, it just becomes a glorified smoke detector. Whenever a door opens in my house—the front door, or even the door to downstairs—the old alarm sounds three annoying beeps. I jumped out of bed and went to the closet for my gun, realizing that it wasn't loaded. I must have been standing just behind the door to my room, because when it opened suddenly I caught it right in the side of the head.

I barely had a chance to moan before a hand grabbed me and dragged me into the living room, sitting me down hard on the couch and attacking me with a piercing bright light. When my eyes adjusted I was looking at a face like a slab of meat.

"You Itchy Crane?"

"Not even sure you got the right guy?"

I got a slap in the face for that.

"Don't get smart with me. I don't like smart guys."

"What, they make you feel dumb?"

I caught another slap for that, one that broke my drunk's rude awakening and brightened me up enough to take an interest in the speaker.

"You gonna cut out that smart lip?"

I pondered the question, taking advantage of the opportunity to look at the five-foot, three-hundred-pound side of beef standing in my living room. I was thinking maybe I could take the bastard when a tall, cool character came drifting in from the kitchen, eating a salami sandwich and chewing it loudly. "Just cover him, Al, lemme do the talking."

Of course there would have to be two. Thugs always come in twos in the funny pages. I thought I'd say nothing for a change.

"Nice digs you got here," the cool one said. He was dark-haired but fair-skinned, with a high Irish forehead and chiseled features. He didn't look dangerous from a physical standpoint, but the Colt in Al's hand made me forget about trying to take either of them.

"Glad you like the place," I said, pressing my fingers to my temples to try to clear my mind of the buzzing sound from either the bourbon or Al's fist, or both. "Why don't you make yourself a sandwich or something—you know, make yourself at home."

"Thanks, I will."

"Want me to slap him again?"

"I don't think that will be necessary." The cool one had a voice like a lizard licking sandpaper. He slithered onto the other couch, stuffed the last of my salami in his mouth, and put his feet on my coffee table. "So, Itchy— can I call you Itchy?"

"Why not."

"Right. Why not. I think we have the upper hand here. So, Itchy, you working this Ashley thing or aren't ya?" He smacked his lips and licked a bit of mustard off a long, pointed index finger.

"Naw, I can't say I'm working it. Floundering is probably the better term."

"Ah. Witty."

"Yeah, real sense of humor this guy's got," Al said, waving the Colt in my general direction.

"Al, why don't you park your Samoan ass."

Samoan. Of course. Why not a Samoan?

Al sat down heavily in one of my chairs, still within slapping distance.

"See, this is the thing here, Itchy. We don't want you working, floundering, investigating, nosing around, sniffing about, wishy-washing, dillydallying—you can invent your own word here, if you like. Let's just say we don't want you doing anything with this Ashley thing. We think we're just fine without you."

"Fine by me," I said, a little too quickly. "Feel like getting the hell out of my house now?"

"Okay, Al, now you can slap him."

He did. It was less a slap than what you would call a full-on, closed-fist punch to the eyebrow. I failed to enjoy it.

"I don't want you to think I don't like you," the lizard was lisping when the stars cleared out of my eyes. "I mean, I like you quite a bit. You've got spunk. Panache. *Je ne sais quoi*. And I like your taste in cold cuts. So what I want, and when I say want, I don't mean want so much as—what's the word, Al?"

"Order?"

"No, that's much too harsh. Ah . . . what I . . . require— there we go—what I require is that you go back to bed, get up in the morning, put a steak on that eye of yours, go out to the store, and buy yourself some more of that nice salami. Maybe I'll pop by next week for a sandwich and we can chat about the weather. Or the '9ers. Or the price of fucking tea in China." He stood up and leaned into me, his hot breath inches from my face. "But what we will NOT talk about is a little cunt named Ashley. Because SHE," he flicked a finger at my eyebrow, which was already beginning to swell, "IS"—flick—"NOT"—flick—"YOUR"—flick—"PROBLEM." He sat down. "We solid on this, Itchy?"

"Sure as you got salami breath, buddy."

Al clocked me a slap across the head. It was half-assed for him, but it brought those constellations right back for me.

"Let it go, Al. Our bright boy here has lots to think about."

I heard those three beeps again and the door shut. I opened my eyes. I heard an engine rev and jumped up, leaned over the back of the couch, parted the Venetians and saw brake lights on a beat-up old Datsun. I copped the license plate number and flopped down on the couch.

Home sweet home, sweet solitude, just me and fifty old ladies screaming bloody murder inside my head.

6

I woke with my head pounding and venom in my veins. I was pissed. I was hired for an impossible job, I was making a damn good effort regardless, and yet I was being subjected to dead bodies and getting battered around and no one was telling me why. I wanted some answers, one way or another, even if I did decide to make the smart move and keep the twenty-five grand and get off the case.

I considered cracking open every phone in the house to see if they really were tapped, but the line could be tapped at another junction. Anyway, if someone wanted to hear what I was saying, it made more sense to simply not be worth hearing. How long before someone else banged on my door in the middle of the night? Better to play it cool. Whether or not that hinky letter was really from Ashley, I needed to be careful.

I hopped in the shower, careful not to catch my reflection in the mirror. The hot water stung my face and I held a cloth to my eye and bathed with one hand. I got out and went to the kitchen for ice and held it to my brow while I called my bank.

McCaffrey's check had cleared.

I was so ecstatic I called the Starbucks at the truck stop and offered the pimply faced kid a twenty to deliver me a Venti Vanilla Latte and spent the next two hours working the phone, Ashley or no Ashley, banal call after banal call. I called Pac Bell, the electric company, the gas company, and the water company, and paid all my over-due balances. Then I called my maxed-out credit card companies and paid them all off too. I was in the black and it felt pretty good.

But I was still pissed, so I went down to the range.

Charlie was a little surprised to see me. "Back again so soon?"

"I told you, it's been a weird week."

She darted a look at my shiner. "What's catching your eye today?" She grinned.

"Cute. Lemme try that nine mil again."

"Thought you said it was too much like a toy."

"Yeah, but it's starting to grow on me."

I popped off a few and my breathing leveled out. By the time I walked out and started Delores, I had made up my mind.

I went back to the Dalton Gallery; I had to take a look.

There were a couple of cop cars parked outside, and the gallery had a sign out front saying that the show had ended early. Some cops were on their way out, but artists and buyers were milling in and out unmolested. I slipped in. Dalton's office was roped off with bright yellow crime scene tape but his body was nowhere to be seen. Not that I would have seen it anyway. Dalton's previously immaculate office was torn to pieces—the file cabinets were emptied and overturned, the desk was on its side, even the framed and glassed-in prints hanging on the wall were smashed. It looked like a hurricane had hit the tiny isolated spot, wreaked its havoc, and escaped out the window. Someone had come back; nothing had been askew when I found Dalton's body other than the chair he'd been sitting in.

I heard a familiar slimy voice down the hall and took a couple steps into the gallery. The lean lizard son of a bitch from the night before was smoothly arguing with a pale blond woman as he bent down over a canvas, slitting it off the stretcher bar with a penknife.

"You can't—you can't!" she protested, and he answered her, as calm as can be, "I bought it, didn't I? It's mine. I can do what I want." It was Ashley's portrait of me. I ducked out before he caught sight of me.

I was almost out the door when I saw something I'd missed before—a gallery guide of the current exhibition. I slipped it into my pocket.

Serena was sitting on the curb, half a block away, crying her eyes out. I sat down next to her and she didn't complain.

"Serena," I said cautiously, "how are you holding up?"

She looked up at me with barren, tear-streaked, beautiful green eyes. "How did you—oh." She recognized me. I was almost hoping she wouldn't. "You were here yesterday."

"That's right." I let her soak that in for a minute. She seemed to be composing herself a bit. "What happened?"

"They killed him!" This came out like projectile vomiting and preceded another torrent of tears and sobs. I put an arm across her shoulder and she melted into me, quaking and quivering.

As she collected herself I tried another approach.

"Serena, I know this is hard, but I need you to tell me what happened yesterday."

"Are you a cop?" Again, those brilliantly sheened green eyes. "I told the cops already."

"I'm not a cop. Just a friend of Mr. Dalton's."

"I . . . my boyfriend was in town from Fresno, and I wanted to see him, just for five minutes, coz I haven't seen him in a month and he just drove in and I wasn't off work yet, so Mr. Dalton let me go."

"Right, I remember."

"But when I came back, this guy was locking the front door. He said Mr. Dalton had to leave, and he was locking up for him—he said he was a business associate. I—I didn't think . . . I was just so happy to leave and see my boyfriend."

"What did this guy look like? Medium height, dark, sharkskin suit?"

"Yeah. You saw him?"

"Only for a minute. What else?"

"That's all. I just . . . It's all my fault!" More water-works, more holding the shivering bird.

"It's not your fault, Serena. You couldn't have done anything. If you had stayed, you'd probably be dead too. It's okay." I held her a minute more and she seemed to calm down for good. "Is your boyfriend still in town?"

"Uh-huh."

"Go see him. You'll be fine. Want me to call you a cab?"

"No . . . it's close."

Something came to me. "You still have a job, right?"

"Mr. Dalton's sister is taking over. She said we'll re-open in a week or so."

"That blond woman inside?"

"Uh-huh."

"Thank you, Serena." I handed her my card. "Listen, if you think of anything else, anything at all, please call me. Call me before you call the cops."

"Why?"

"Because the cops won't find the killer."

"How do you know?"

"Because they don't know why he killed him."

"Do you?" Those green eyes hit me like an interrogation spotlight.

"No. But I'm going to find out."

I figured Dalton's sister would be easy to find and would manage to stay alive for a while. I didn't want to wear out my welcome and risk running into Mr. Salami Eater. Just seeing that lizard slice my portrait off its frame made me angry all over again. I could have simply turned him in to the cops—he'd been in my house, he had to know something. But getting him picked up wouldn't get me anywhere.

I had to find Ashley. Maybe McCaffrey had hired me to do his dirty laundry, but this was quickly becoming something else. I had to know why Ashley was painting me. I had to know who she was.

I had to find Al.

I walked over to Powell and Market, by the cable car stop, and hit a pay phone in the midst of swarming tourists to call my old friend Shelley at the San Mateo DMV.

"David?" I could hear the smile creeping up the sides of her pouty lips. "Is that you?"

"It's me, Shelley."

"So when are we going out?"

I'd been baiting Shelley ever since I first started asking her for favors. I think she knew it was never going to happen, but I had to keep up the charade. It was the silently agreed-upon game. "Next week. For sure. I'll give you a call."

"I bet you will. Where you been? I haven't heard from you in *aaaa*ges." She dragged that last bit out. Someone sometime must have told her it was cute.

"Oh, you know, here, there."

"Uh-huh. Hold on a minute." She cupped a hand over the receiver and her voice came through a little muffled. "I *am* talking to a customer. Just a minute." She cleared up again. "I'm back. What can I do for you, Mr. Crane?"

I gave her Al's license plate number and asked her to get me everything she could.

"I'll need a couple hours. Give me your cell phone number, I'll call you back when I get it."

"Shelley, I don't have a cell phone."

She sucked a little air through her teeth. "You just don't want to give me the number." She was cute, you had to hand it to her.

"No, sweety, I really don't have a cell, and I won't be home until long after you get off work. I'll call you back by the end of the day."

I grabbed a slice at Blondie's, walked back to Delores, drove her home, and went upstairs to try to take a nap, but sleep wouldn't come. I remembered the gallery guide and dug it out, spreading it across my knees and reading it in bed like an invalid.

The exhibition was a group show of Bay Area 2D artists, and the only other common element was that all submissions had to be six feet by five feet. I hadn't noticed at the gallery, hadn't looked closely at any work but Ashley's—a rookie move. Most were oils, some were ink, some acrylic, but they were all on canvas, six by five. The gallery wanted to explore the possibilities of artists unafraid to work on a large scale, blah blah blah . . . bios of the artists. Ashley's read like a ransom note from another dimension:

> Ashley is not: an acronym or an anagram. Ashley does not: work with acrylic, steel, or clay. Ashley will not: sell out or fade away. Ashley was born, is living, and will someday die. Ashley admits to being fixated on one particular subject matter. It's a phase. Enjoy.

It made me shiver, it made me understand all the more why she drove Dalton crazy. I reached down and absently stuck the guide under my mattress, and tried again to fade away to dreamland. No dice.

But I knew what was bothering me. It was staring me in the face and I couldn't look away. That was why I couldn't drop the case. It had nothing to do with McCaffrey's twenty-five Gs, it had nothing to do with two thugs sticking a gun in my face.

It was Ashley.

Why the hell was this girl painting portraits of me? How did she know what I looked like? How the devil did she know where I was on New Year's Day? How did Al and Lizard and Sharkskin seem to know more about this than me? *Fixated on one particular subject matter*—how many more of these paintings were there?

I'd lived in San Francisco long enough to get my fill

of new age theologies, crackpot philosophies, and cock-amamie mystical ideas about the universe. I'd heard about astral projection, tantra, the Kabbalah, ESP—it was all a load of hooey. But this . . . this was too weird. What could explain it? Was I next on *The X-Files*? Was this young girl somehow tapped into my mind? Could she see me from a distance? Did she dream about me, and paint her dreams like Dali?

I remembered an article I'd read about remote view-ing, a paranormal, ESP method of seeing something hid-den from view, or something happening very far away. The phenomenon was explored at the Stanford Research Institute in the seventies and later funded by the CIA. The government's twenty-million-dollar research program—with the unlikely name of the Stargate Project—was shut down, and documents were declassified a couple of years back. The scientific debate was predictable: pro-ponents swore it worked and that valuable information could be gained; detractors called it pseudoscience and either said that more research was required or that it was a straight-up hoax. The truly spooky part is that proponents imply that RV is a technique that can be taught and learned by anyone, psychic or not. It doesn't take an extraordinary amount of paranoia to wonder if the CIA is still fooling around with mind tricks, but my own paranoia begs the question: why would a young girl, even a CIA operative, be spying on me? Everything about it sent a creeping skeletal hand up the back of my spine.

Somehow it would be easier to accept if she lived in Wisconsin and had no idea that the paintings she was cranking out depicted reality, but that note . . . if it really did come from Ashley, my Ashley, then she knew who I was and how to find me. She lived in California, somewhere—or did until recently. She hadn't disappeared; she was hiding from someone.

I convinced myself that if I could fall asleep I would have a dream about Ashley, and we would trade secrets and make love and take the extra twenty-five grand and rent a house in Belize and grow old together, dreaming each other's dreams. . .

7

I woke in the late afternoon and walked down to the Schoolhouse Deli to use the pay phone. Shelley had a name for me, Alan Punihaole—sounded more Hawaiian than Samoan—and a San Francisco address. I went home and waited out the evening.

I got out my World War II–issue .45 automatic pistol, a Colt M1911A1, and loaded it up, strapped on a shoulder holster, and slipped on a black blazer. I took a wooden box down from the top of the closet and found my first gun, a model 7 two-shot Derringer that I'd bought at a flea market many years back. It was a .38—a pretty big gun for a dainty little peashooter. I rigged it to my ankle with an old leather belt. I went rummaging in the kitchen drawers and found a box cutter—a simple razor blade in a small plastic sheath, the kind that you have to be eighteen to buy now that gangs are using them as weapons. I broke off the end to expose a fresh, sharp blade.

Around eleven I caught the last bus to the Colma station and rode the BART to Civic Center. I walked down 7th and onto a shitty industrial block past Harrison, almost underneath the 80 overpass. Punihaole was on the buzzer list, third floor. I rang the buzzer above his: *Durkett*. An elderly female voice squawked at me: "Hello?"

I tried to lower mine into a drawl. "Sorry, Mrs. Durkett, it's Al downstairs, my key don't work."

"Asshole," she muttered, but buzzed me in. Al seemed to make an impression on everyone.

I walked up the three flights and was happy to learn that his was the only apartment on the floor. I could hear a television humming quietly on the other side of the door. I peeked up and down the staircase one last time and drew my .45, then tapped the door lightly and stepped aside.

Fortunately, Al wasn't a cautious kind of guy. He threw the door open and, not seeing anyone, stuck his fat face out. I shoved my .45 into his pug nose. "Get in, moron, and don't make a fucking peep." He didn't. I shut the door behind us and locked it without taking my eyes or my gun off him. He was in his bathrobe but still started up tough.

"What are you, fuckin' stupid? I know where you live."

"And I know where you live, Punihaole. Shut up, and turn that TV up a couple notches." He turned it up almost to blaring. Mrs. Durkett immediately started banging on the floor above us. "Not so loud, asshole, I don't want Durkett calling the cops." He shot me a wicked glare and turned it down.

The room was dingy, if not altogether filthy. The couch was folded out. There was another room in the back but I could see it was empty. "Where's your roommate?"

"Kicked him out."

"Why don't you sleep in the back?"

He shrugged. "I like it out here."

"That's fine, Alan. Take off the bathrobe."

"What?"

"You forget what this is?" I waggled the .45. "Take it off." He dropped the robe, exposing Daffy Duck boxer shorts and a grayed wife beater. "Nice shorts, Alan."

"Don't call me—"

"What? Dead?" That got him. "Right. Drop the Daffys and lay down on the hide-a-bed."

"What?"

"Fucking do it, Alan, I don't have all night to sit around watching *Seinfeld*."

"What are you, some kinda fag?"

"I bet you get by real well in this city with that attitude. You got it, Alan, I'm some kind of fag and I came over to blow you at gunpoint. Do it."

His face was a pinched melon of embarrassment as he took off his boxers. The sagging rolls of fat just about covered his excuse for manhood. He lay down on his stomach, the couch offering up loud springy complaints. I put my right foot solidly against the back of his neck, holding the .45 steady to his nose.

"Put yer cock in my mouth and I'll bite it off."

"They teach you that in prison, Alan? Trust me, I have no such ideas. I'm just gonna cut yours off." With that I took out the box cutter, snicked it open, and locked it in place.

His eyes grew wide as two moons and he was surprisingly silent.

"Now," I said, reaching back with the cutter, "I can't reach too well and still hold the heat on you, so please forgive me if I miss the first couple of times. Besides," I grinned, "I'm a little clumsy with my left hand." I pressed the blade to a fat thigh and he twitched and opened up.

"What do you want? Please please please, what do you want?"

"I want to cut your nuts off, you fat fuck. I don't like being assaulted and I want you to remember that."

"Please, anything."

"Where's Ashley, Alan?"

"I don't know! You gotta believe me. I don't even know who Ashley is!"

"Bullshit." I made a clumsy swipe and grazed him, just enough to scare him. He was howling.

"I don't know!"

"Quiet down. Who hired you to slap me around?"

"I don't know that either! I swear it!"

I pushed the .45 hard into his nose, so hard that he turned his face to the side, and I reached over and quickly cut him with the blade again, higher up. He started bawling like a little girl.

"Talk to me, Alan. It's way past my bedtime and I'm getting cranky."

"Conrad hired me! I don't know nothing else!"

"Who the fuck is Conrad?"

"The guy from last night. He just hires me when he needs some extra muscle or he wants me to drive him around—coz he don't drive."

I tapped him on the side of the head with the gun and reached over again, but he was already flinching. "*Doesn't* drive, Alan. What, is English not your first language?"

"Conrad doesn't drive! Conrad doesn't drive!"

"What's his last name?"

"Jones, C-Conrad Jones."

"And who hired Conrad?"

"I don't knoooow!" He was starting to squeal and looked like he was about to wet himself. He didn't know anything.

"All right, Alan. Pull up your shorts." I drew back a bit so he could look at me. His pupils were pinholes as he wriggled the Daffys up his fat thighs. "Where can I find Conrad?"

"I . . . I don't know."

"Where does he live? What's his phone number?"

"I don't know. I shoot pool in the afternoons at Hollywood Billiards. He finds me there."

"You've never picked him up at his house?"

"No, I swear it. He's super secret. Jones ain't even his real name, somebody tole me."

So much for trying Shelley at the DMV. "What else do you know about him?"

"Just that he's always eatin' and he's always skinny."

I knew that much. We were done. "You did good, Alan. I'm real proud of you. I'm gonna let you keep that little pecker of yours."

He exhaled deeply and sat up, swinging his feet onto the floor. "Thanks," he wheezed, devoid of sarcasm.

"But I need two more things from you."

"What?"

"Number one: you owe me a favor. I don't know what it is yet, but one of these days I'm going to walk into Hollywood Billiards and you're going to say, *What can I do for you, Mr. Crane?* Got that?"

"S-sure. You got it."

"And the second thing: don't you *ever*"—I leaned in

and hacked him a good one through the Daffys—"fuck with me again or I *will* chop your balls off. You'll get man titties that make these"—I nosed the gun at his chest— "look buff." He grabbed his thigh, bit his lip, and gave me the look of a fat kid who just had his lunch money stolen. "You tell anyone I was here and it's"—I whispered close to his ear—"*snick snick.*"

I moved to the door. He had one hand on his wound and one over his wet eyes.

"Hey Alan," I said, "Conrad called you Samoan, but Punihaole? That sounds Hawaiian to me."

"What do you care?" He was blubbering.

"Al . . . this isn't personal. This is business. You fucked with me, I gotta fuck with you. It doesn't mean we can't be friends. I'm starting to like you." He didn't answer but seemed to calm down a little. "Seriously. Punihaole?"

"My mom's name was Tuitama. She's Samoan. My dad's Hawaiian: Punihaole."

I grinned at him. "So your dad likes big women, huh?" He didn't say anything, but stifled a grin. "What'd you do tonight, Alan?"

"I—I stayed home and watched TV."

"Good boy, Al. I'll be seeing you."

I let myself out.

I walked back to Market and down to Gough to catch a cab. No one saw me walk out of Al's place and that was dandy by me. I felt good, almost too good, like I had gotten away with something but didn't quite know what. I had crossed a line somewhere. I was in it now, there was no getting out. But since Ashley was painting creepy snapshots of my life, I guess I was always in it. The fact that I didn't know *what* I was into no longer made any difference.

I sat on the left side of the cab and rolled down the window and looked out at my bay . . . I was becoming the part, I realized. I'd always been a quick study, and the way Conrad Jones—if that was his name—had worked me over taught me exactly how to get at big Al. There wasn't a twinge of regret in my bones for the way I had frightened him, terrorized him, threatened him. Any asshole who hung around a pool hall waiting to get hired as a thug deserved what he got.

But I still had nothing. My only real lead—the gallery— was dead as Dalton. I didn't know how Al and Conrad had caught on to me but it didn't matter—Al didn't know his ass from a hole in the ground and Conrad wouldn't be as easy to intimidate. He was clearly the brains of the team and wouldn't crack easily. Al was just a big dope gone astray, but Conrad . . . something about the way he cut the canvas off the stretcher, the way he barked at Susan. . . He was the worst kind of man—one incapable of remorse.

I had the cab let me out at 101 and Grand Ave. and walked the rest of the way home. I chain-smoked until I was out, thinking about it all.

8

The next morning I woke up hacking and took a long, hot shower. I whipped up a quick breakfast of poached eggs on toast and went back to square one: the painting in my garage. I looked at it for a solid hour but saw nothing I hadn't seen before. Me, the barber, the signature, the date . . . it was good brushwork, good composition, and a good likeness, but I'm not an art critic. I'm an info guy, and the information I needed was, where is the artist?

I went down to the Schoolhouse Deli and worked the pay phone.

"Good morning, Dalton Gallery, this is Susan Dalton, can I help you?"

"Susan, hello. My name's David Crane."

"And what can I do for you?"

"I'm sorry to bring up a difficult subject, but I was in the gallery the other day. The day your brother, ah . . ."

There was a stiff pause on the line. "I see. And what exactly do you want?"

"I don't want to trouble you, Miss Dalton, but I was hoping I could come down and ask you a few questions."

"I've already told the police everything—"

"I'm not with the police, Miss Dalton, I'm a journalist, and it would be a big help to me if you could spare a few moments. Can I come down this afternoon?"

"I can't . . . I can't talk about it here, it's too—"

"Let me buy you lunch."

She chewed that over. "All right. Meet me at Zuni at one o'clock."

Expensive taste, but the hell with it. I was a rich man.

I was there early, fiddling with a fork as a surrogate cigarette and eyeing the door. Susan came striding in about a quarter past the hour, looking very smart in a skirt and a suit jacket, her blond hair pulled back severely, dark shades on her face. She had the same thin lips as her brother, but on her face they lent an air of elegance and mystery, like she knew something but you'd have to beg to get it out of her. Seeing her for the second time, I realized what I hadn't quite noticed the day before at the gallery: she was hot stuff. The conservative clothes couldn't hide the voluptuous body straining against the fabric.

I caught her at the bar and fumbled through my introduction, showing her to the table. I was relieved when she said she wanted a drink, and we ordered Bloody Marys and I grabbed the bull by the horns and ordered a dozen oysters—Malpeques, Kumamotos, and Wellfleets. Turned out she had been a freelance journalist before getting into telecommunications and had done gigs over at the *Chronicle*, so we cut up and cracked jokes about my old cronies, laughing like college kids. She was getting comfortable and I thought if I could get her at ease it would all go smoothly. After a mutual laugh at the expense of one of my drunk ex-editors, she got strangely quiet.

"David."

"Yeah."

"I'm sorry . . . about what happened to you with the *Guardian*."

"Oh . . . you heard about that."

"Yes. I didn't recognize your name at first, but when you were talking about . . . Anyway, I put it together."

I shrugged. "You live, you die."

"I'm really sorry."

"Forget it."

"I hope you don't blame yourself."

"It's done. Really." I signaled the waiter just to change the subject, but our food was already coming. We ate quietly, stealing glances at one another. I thought I felt her stockinged leg brush mine, but I was sure it was my imagination.

When we both had frothy cappuccinos in front of us, I opened it up: "How familiar are you with the workings of your brother's gallery?"

She shifted in her seat. "I was Jeffrey's . . . unofficial consultant from the very beginning. I know nothing about art, but I know a thing or two about business, and I know how to deal with people. Jeffrey . . . was not a people person."

"He lived alone, I take it?"

"Yes. He had a lover every now and then—he was gay, I guess you knew that. But the gallery was really his life. It was all he thought about. He loved art, he hated artists, and he couldn't get enough of either."

"Do you have any idea why he might have been killed? Did he have any enemies, any—"

"No. Really, I haven't a clue. This whole thing has been like a roller-coaster ride. I'm trying to get his affairs in order, our parents are coming out for the service, and meanwhile I'm trying to keep his gallery from going under. That's all he would have wanted."

I let that linger a bit, taking in the ambience of the fading lunchtime rush. She sipped her cappuccino and set it down with long, slender fingers. "Susan, what do you know about an artist named Ashley?"

She gave me a wan, sympathetic grin. "I had forgotten about her until that awful man came in yesterday to pick up her painting. But Jeffrey mentioned her several times—she drove him crazy. *All* the artists drove him crazy, but Ashley especially. He thought she was incredibly talented, but she always painted the same subject, and he thought she would be difficult to sell. And she wouldn't take any advice from him at all. He called her 'the diva.' I never met her, but I think he discovered her at a group show or something. She had a studio . . . somewhere. I forget."

"Listen, anything you could find out about her would be a fantastic help. I think—"

"Wait a minute. It's you, isn't it? That painting at the gallery—it's you."

"It did look a bit like me. But I'm sure it's just a coincidence."

She leveled a steamy gaze at me and for a moment I imagined her Marin attire matted up on my bathroom floor. "Mm-hmm."

"I promise you," I said in my most convincing voice, "I've never met her."

"So what is it? You think Ashley had something to do with Jeffrey's death? I thought it must be that man Serena saw—"

"I think it was. But yes, I think it has something to do with Ashley."

"Why?"

I took a deep breath. "I don't want to tell you too much, Susan, and to be honest, I don't know that much. But Ashley's gone missing. I was hired to find her. I discovered that she had a piece at your brother's gallery and went to talk to him. Half an hour later he was . . ."

"Dead. I see."

"Susan, you don't seem all that troubled—"

"Jeffrey tested positive for HIV years ago. He went into full-blown AIDS about six months back. The cocktails weren't really helping, his health was deteriorating slowly but steadily . . . I've had some time to deal with the possibility of his death. Perhaps it's better this way."

"I'm sorry."

"We're all sorry."

I thought about that. "Did Jeffrey keep files, or any kind of background information on his artists?"

She shook her head. "He did, he was quite good about it, but they were all destroyed or went missing when . . ." She trailed off.

"Right. I saw the office."

She said nothing. We were drifting away from each other like continents.

I paid the check and gave her my card. "If anything turns up—anything—or if you think of anything . . ."

"I will." She laid that gaze on me again and I excused myself quickly.

* * *

When Susan called later that night I hoped it was social.

"David? This may sound a little forward, but—"

"I'm sorry, can I call you back in just a few minutes?" *Don't hang up, gorgeous, my phone is tapped.* She didn't speak at first and I didn't breathe.

"Um . . . sure."

She gave me her number and I ran down the street to the pay phone and called her back, almost panting.

"Can you come over?"

My heart did a double take but it clearly wasn't a booty call. She lived in the Marina; I had to forgive her for that. Yuppies come in all shapes and sizes. I found a parking space on Chestnut and walked up Bay and found her little complex and rang the bell. She answered the door in a comfortable little sundress that left absolutely nothing to the imagination—or perhaps too much. Mine was running wild.

"I'm so glad you came by. I found something, and it just made me so nervous that I—it sounds stupid, but I just didn't want to tell you about it over the phone." It didn't sound stupid to me.

"Show me."

She showed me a portable file cabinet, one of those plastic things you get at the Container Store. "I was at Jeffrey's apartment. He had a small place in the Castro. I was just going through some things and I found this. It was weird—it was stuck in the back of the closet, kind of hidden." She was getting herself all worked up into a cute frenzy. "I'm sorry—I'm terrible. Can I get you something?"

I settled on a Sierra Nevada and she sat me down at an Ikea table. The apartment was small but tastefully decorated: rich, plush, off-white carpet, family photos, a television that wasn't quite the center of attention. I figured the kitchen would have china that matched the curtains, and the sheets on her bed probably matched her underwear.

Turns out Dalton was less of a gallery owner than an artist cultivator. He coached his artists and pushed them in directions he found appropriate, and kept intricate files on each of them.

"This is the one I wanted you to see."

The file, a slim manila folder, was labeled simply, *Ashley*, and contained a number of neat, handwritten field notes, for lack of a better term. It was beautiful . . . Dalton, that wonderful, perfidious son of a bitch, had mapped out his brain for us. I skimmed over it for the highlights:

> *Went to show at Project Artaud, 499 Alabama—bullshit Mission School ilk. Collaboration between Jason Masello and the mononymous "Ashley." Calling it "collaboration" is a travesty; they're each doing their own thing and apparently hating each other for it. Probably lovers hoping to find a common ground—and failing. Masello is an idiot. Ashley Fenn is a genius.*

I jumped. "Fenn? That's her last name?"

Susan nodded. "I think so. But look at this," Susan said, flipping past a copy of the gallery guide with a couple photos, descriptions of the works, and another bizarre bio of our Ashley to direct me to another page of Dalton's notes: *Finally went to Ashley's studio in Bayview.*

"Bayview? Pretty rough neighborhood for a young girl."

"Keep reading."

Finally went to Ashley's studio in Bayview. Took a long time to convince her to let me come—she swore me to secrecy, to never tell anyone where it was. Strange—not convinced it WAS her studio—it looked like she brought finished works into an empty space. No sign of any work actually being done there. Regardless, can't believe one so young has such command of brush, palette, and composition. Like she was born with it. She has a fine eye, is an obsessive observer. You can feel her watching you, it's almost creepy. Wanted to offer her a solo show immediately, but every painting is a portrait of the same man. Some are complex enough to not be considered just portraits, but . . . no. Encouraged her to branch out; she was indignant. Conversation was strained and difficult. Asked her who the subject was and she said she didn't know. "I see him in my dreams." Bullshit. He has to be a lover or a crush. They're too good, too consistent. She knows him from life—or a thousand photographs. I said, "These are paintings to die for," and she laughed and said, "They really are. You have no idea." Woman needs a shrink and a prescription.

I looked up at Susan, who was hovering over me expectantly. I hoped she couldn't see the hairs on the back of my neck standing at attention. She put a hand on the back of my chair. "*Paintings to die for,*" she said. "That gave me the creeps."

"Me too." There was more but I couldn't concentrate. "Susan, let me have this."

"David, I'd like to, but I think I should give it to the police. Look at the last page in the file."

I skipped ahead.

Convinced Ashley to give me a piece for the 5x6 group show. You would think she didn't want to sell anything. She insisted on absolute secrecy, still won't tell me her last name—I didn't divulge that Masello already leaked it. She said, "These paintings could get me killed." I told her she was being overly dramatic. She grabbed me, very disconcerting, and made me promise I wouldn't tell anyone about her studio or her other work. "This is nitroglycerin. You can't tell anyone about me. I'm a dangerous girl." I'm sure it's all in her mind but a promise is a promise. She's unbalanced, and I worry she could easily become unhinged. I wonder if she was abused. Before I left she asked if I thought all our dreams came true in heaven. I told her I hoped so, and she said, "Bless you" and gave me a haunted look. What a nut job.

"Susan," I said, "just give me two days with this before you go to the police. All right? Let me make a copy. I want to talk to this Masello character before the cops get to him and spook him for real."

"All right," she said, nodding. "Take it."

I finished my beer and was on my way out when something about the way she was fingering the strap on her dress made me pause.

"What?" she asked, looking at me with radiance, her head slightly askew. "What are you looking at?"

"Nothing." I took her face in my hands and kissed her—a deep, soul-destroying kiss that lasted half an hour and took us into the bedroom. We made furtive, silent love for what seemed like a week. The sheets didn't match her underwear; she wasn't wearing any.

9

The cop at the door made me jump until I realized it was only Michael, a South City radio-car cop who grew up across the street and often comes by to visit his parents, a sweet couple, Chinese immigrants.

"Hey, Michael, how are you?"

"Can I come in?"

"Please." I pushed open the screen.

"Can we sit? This is business, David."

I sat him down in the kitchen and offered him the stale coffee that had been in the pot since the day before. He refused. I poured myself a cup—it was still early, I'd come in late from Susan's, and I felt like I'd slept for about twenty minutes. The coffee was terrible but still coffee.

"Listen, David, I'm here on about six favors, so I really need you to be straight up with me."

"What favors?" I was just waiting to hear the name Ashley.

"I got a call from an SF inspector. Something tied in to South City, and they wanted me to pick up a possible perp/possible witness, and bring him in for questioning."

I sat down across from him, sipped my coffee, and waited. He gave me that cop look. I relented. "And?"

"You know a woman named Susan Dalton?"

My heart was in my throat and I didn't want it to go back down. "Yes, I know her. Why?"

"Neighbors thought they heard a gunshot in her building last night. Susan was in her bed with a bullet under the chin."

I stood up quickly. "Oh, fuck no." I went to the sink and leaned over it. This was all my fault, somehow. That poor, wonderful, sweet girl.

"Apparently it was pretty messy."

I glared at him. "Save me the details, will you?"

"Sorry. How did you know her, exactly? See, they found your business card in her apartment. You'll have to go downtown and make a statement."

I shook my head and stared at the errant Cheerios circling in the bottom of the drain. "I . . . I went to this art show south of Market. There was a big hubbub because . . . apparently the owner was shot. Susan's brother. Anyway, I met her there, and . . . guess you could say I was seeing her."

"The guys said she was pretty hot."

"Yeah." I wanted to hit him. "You could say that."

"You fuck her?"

"With all due respect, officer, fuck you and your mother."

"Hey, David, I'm just trying to save you some trouble. It's gonna come out. They did the preliminary autopsy this morning and they found semen in her."

Susan had these condoms that were like circus balloons. One broke, and after the initial freakout, when we confirmed that we were both clean and that she was on the pill, we giggled about it and the second time didn't use anything at all.

"Yeah," I confessed, "that would be mine."

"Rawdoggin' it, huh?"

His smirk made me want to hurt him. He caught my look and I didn't have to say anything.

"Well, listen, I'm no inspector, but I'm guessing you were the last person—well, second-to-last—to see her alive. You gotta go down and make a statement. I don't think you're really a suspect or they would have come to get you already. Just be honest about what time you left and hope it clears you from the estimated time of death."

"Thanks so much for your concern and consideration."

He stood up then and came over and put a hand on my shoulder. "I'm sorry, man." I liked him for that. "But David, tell me one thing." I hated him all over again. "Were you working something?"

"What do you mean?"

"Come on. I told you when you first started this business that you were going to turn into some kind of private dick. Were you working something?"

"No." I looked at him slow and steady, like I was trying to guess whether or not he had a flush to beat my full house. "Just having a good time with a sweet lady."

"All right. I won't ask again." He handed me a business card for an SF inspector at the Northern District Police Station, in the Western Addition. "You gotta go talk to these guys. If they have to come get you it's gonna look bad. Take it easy, David."

"Yeah, thanks."

I poured a drink and called the number on the card and told a secretary I was on my way. Guess I knew when this whole thing started that sooner or later I'd be sitting in a police station lying my ass off.

Inspector Berrera was a large, quiet man of obvious Hispanic decent. He seemed to eschew speaking for grunts, gestures, and other silent expressions that gave off the impression that he was wise—or at least pensive. Inspector Willits was smaller, in excellent shape, talked more, and was generally more animate. In the good-cop, bad-cop archetype, neither fell into either category comfortably, but I was willing to give myself the benefit of the doubt and consider them both bad cops.

The lying took up most of the afternoon. I wish they'd give cops secretaries; I've never seen a slower one-finger typist. Willits paced and fidgeted with a coffee cup like an ex-smoker; Berrera hunted, pecked, and gave me Cro-Magnon stares.

"How well did you know Susan Dalton?" Willits asked.

"We just met, inspector."

"She was naked when they found her. That your juice in her?"

Perverts. I never met a cop who wasn't. "Yes. I'm happy to take a blood test."

"We'll get to that. Did you know her brother was murdered just a few days ago?"

"I did."

"What do you think about that?" Willits stopped fidgeting for a moment and Berrera swung his enormous head to face me.

"Was that a question, inspector?"

Berrera didn't like that and grunted loudly. Willits

flared his nostrils and nearly spat, "What do you think about Dalton and her brother both being murdered?"

"I think it's tragic, inspector. Especially Susan. The brother I didn't know, but Susan I really liked."

"I'll bet you did."

Willits was starting to piss me off, and I wondered if I'd have better luck with Berrera. We could just grunt at each other and I could be on my way. "Why was the brother killed?" I ventured.

"Excuse me?" Willits didn't seem to like having someone else ask questions.

"I'm just curious. Do you think there's a connection between the two murders?"

"You seem pretty calm, Crane."

"I figure if I were a suspect I'd know it by now."

"How did you meet Mrs. Dalton?"

"Miss."

"Excuse me?" So polite, that Willits. A little slow, but the polite part actually put him a cut above most cops I'd had the displeasure of meeting.

"*Miss* Dalton. She wasn't married."

Berrera snapped his jaws. "Stop fucking around."

"I went to Dalton's gallery—the brother's—to see the current show. He had just been killed, there were cops everywhere. I happened to see Susan, I thought she was gorgeous. I called the gallery and expressed condolences and asked her to lunch. We had lunch. I got invited over to her place. Here I am." It was mostly true. I had to admit to being at the scene after Dalton got it, in case I'd been seen, but I couldn't think of a good reason to bring the Ashley element into this.

Berrera chuckled, clacking the keys.

"Regular ambulance chaser, huh?" said Willits. "Always get your dates at crime scenes?"

I let that go. "So do you have any idea why either one of these people were killed?"

"You seem awfully interested—"

"Willits, I make love to a woman and six hours later she's dead. Damn right I'm interested."

That rattled him a bit. "I understand, Crane. But we can't discuss an investigation. I'm sure you understand."

"So why am I here?"

The two cops exchanged a look. They had nothing on me, but they weren't going to give me anything, either.

Willits grabbed a clipboard and flipped a couple pages. He read it off: "Old lady on the ground floor heard you come in. Thought it was late for visitors, but 'you know those young kids.' Got a pretty good look at you, gave a fair description. She stayed up late watching *Perry Mason*, if you can believe it, and heard you leave. Almost immediately heard someone else buzz Ms. Dalton. Footsteps on the stairs, a little commotion, footsteps coming down. Thought it was strange that she didn't hear Dalton's door close. Peeked out and saw a guy leaving—didn't get a good look, but knew it was a different guy." He looked at me from under his eyebrows. "Went upstairs to check on Dalton—you know the rest." He put the clipboard down and picked up his empty coffee cup. "You're not a suspect." Thank god for nosy neighbors. "But we'd like to know what you know. If there's any reason you can think of why anyone would want Ms. Dalton dead."

I spread my hands. "I don't know anything. Like I said, we just met."

Part of me wanted to tell them everything, and a bigger part of me wanted to tell them I was on a case but bait them along so they would keep me abreast of whatever they found out. I wasn't yet convinced that Ashley was the reason the Daltons got killed, but it all looked sufficiently sinister to keep me from dropping her name. All I needed was a couple of cops stumbling around, getting Ashley whacked before I could figure out what was really going on. Clearly, these two had no clue. It never even occurred to them to look at the artists hanging in Dalton's gallery.

Willits handed me his card. "If you think of anything else, give us a call."

"I will."

The pay phone was free, and the lobby of the cop shop was busy enough that I figured no one would notice me. There just wasn't any time to waste.

"The flowers are *beauuuu*-tiful," Shelley said when I got her on the line. I'd called a florist before coming downtown and sent her a bouquet of stargazer lilies— they were powerfully odorous, would make all the ladies at the DMV jealous. "You must need something pretty bad."

"I do, Shelley, and you know I feel awful about pestering you, but this one just won't wait."

"Well, you know the way to a girl's heart." She lowered her voice. "My coworker's on break, so shoot. I'll look it up right now."

I lowered mine. "Ashley Fenn, two *n*'s. Last known in San Francisco, born in LA. Anything you can tell me."

I watched a couple of boys in blue taking out an obviously homeless black woman who didn't seem so keen on being released.

Shelley quietly hummed to herself as her fingernails tapped the keyboard. "Oh."

"Oh what?"

"Oh. She's dead, David."

"What?"

"She's dead. Sorry. You didn't know her, did you?"

"No, no—when did she die?"

"Almost three years ago."

My head was spinning. All of a sudden there were cops everywhere, like a Gonzo nightmare. "I gotta call you back. Wait—what's the last known address?"

"Um . . . 490 Jamestown Avenue. Wait, why does that sound familiar?"

It wasn't fishy, it was a whole can of tuna. "It's not a residence, Shelley. It's the address of Candlestick Park."

I needed a drink, and that drink was going to need a lot of friends.

10

I woke up with my head in a bowling-ball bag, strikes ringing in my ears. I chain-smoked and went over everything I had to look at. I went through McCaffrey's original fax. I dug the gallery guide from Dalton's out from under my mattress and read it over five times to be sure I hadn't missed anything. I read Dalton's file on Ashley and I read it again. If there was one thing about this case that hung together, it was that everyone who came in contact with Ashley thought she was touched—or at the very least a little bit strange. There was nothing else to go on, nothing that I could see with my face pressed so tightly against it. But perhaps Ashley acted strangely for a reason. As the dead bodies piled up, so did reasons to give her the benefit of the doubt.

The smell of Susan's skin was still fresh in my mind, and I couldn't shake the feeling that her murder was on my hands. I could see Sharkskin's grin and almost hear him on my heels. He was a ghost, motives unknowable. The only players I could begin to unravel were Conrad and McCaffrey.

Conrad knew I had been hired to find Ashley, but did he know McCaffrey? If McCaffrey wanted her found and Conrad wanted her lost, they weren't playing for the same team. And either way it didn't compute—whether you wanted Ashley dead or alive, why annihilate the only known connection to her? Was I completely off base in thinking that Ashley was the reason the Daltons were dead? One thing I knew for sure: neither Conrad nor McCaffrey were art collectors. But it tied them together. It all came back to the painting.

Ashley couldn't be dead. Not my Ashley, anyway. Even if it were true—if the woman named Ashley Fenn had been dead for three years—the painting was newer than that. The letter she sent me. The show at Dalton's gallery—even Dalton's notes. This girl, this mysterious creature, whatever her name, was still out there. I could feel her. I could almost smell her.

I had two decent leads: Ashley's old partner in crime, and the painting itself. Jason Masello was easy to find—he was listed. He lived on Hill Street in the Mission, a one-block road between Valencia and Guerrero. And the painting I could take to an art restoration shop I knew in West Portal. I went downstairs to the garage and, taking a page out of Conrad's book, cut the painting off the stretcher. I rolled it up, wrapped it in an old shop tarp, and tossed it in the trunk of my car.

I kept an eye on the rearview all the way to the City, watching for tails. I took the old Army exit—Cesar Chavez now, but always Army to me—and cut into the low, flat panorama of the Mission. I circled the 24th Street BART station, taking in the busy visage of hipsters and Mexicans running errands, voices rattling under the clear sky, the squeak of the 14-Mission lurching to an electric stop, the vague, lingering scent of a taqueria.

I found a parking place on Mission, fed the meter, and walked over to Valencia and 21st, and then up the steep incline of the aptly named Hill Street, my smoker's lungs heaving. I rang the buzzer and waited. I noticed the place had one of those antiquated intercom systems—a hole in the entryway that was essentially a tube leading upstairs. The door led into a stairway, and I saw Masello running down the stairs toward me in baggy, paint-spattered jeans and a grimy concert T-shirt, with long, unkempt hair. He saw me through the glass and stopped a moment, then opened the door a crack.

"Yes?"

"Are you Jason Masello?"

"Who wants to know?"

Smart lad. I showed him my card. "David Crane. Sorry to bother you, I was hoping you might have a minute. I'm working on a story about Ashley, and I understand you used to work with her."

He looked at me over the card in his hand and shook his head. "Ashley. Fuck. Yeah, come on in."

I followed him up the stairs. The apartment was nice, large for one person. We came into a short hallway leading left to the kitchen with a bedroom beyond, or right into a small sitting room with a futon and stacks of records.

"Give me one second." He went through the sitting room to a small room behind it, his studio. I watched from the doorway as he took up a brush and viciously attacked a small canvas on an easel. The piece looked like stale buffalo dung propped up to salute. There were other paintings scattered about the room, more of the same ilk. Abstract, unrecognizable, representative of nothing and suggestive of only black moods and despair. The black paintings of Goya without the skill or precision: pure, fetid ego.

"I just have to finish this glaze before it gets all hard on me."

"No problem." I watched as he covered the canvas top to bottom in wide, even strokes. Now it looked like shellacked buffalo dung. He dropped the brush on a mangy palette and wiped his hands on his pants. He had a wide, sincere face, with expressive brown eyes. He waved me back to the sitting room, and as I entered it with him behind me, I heard a soft click that sounded like glass. He offered me a bottle of water sitting on the table. I declined. He motioned to the futon and we both sat. Near the door to the studio was a small shelf with what looked like a picture frame, facedown.

"What do you want to know about Ash?"

"Anything you can tell me, really. She's proving to be a bit of an enigma."

"Yeah . . . that's her M.O. One of these artists who hopes to get famous by being all mysterious. Like if no one knows who she is or what she's about, everyone will want to buy her stuff." He shrugged. "Guess it's working for her, if you buy into all that bullshit."

"You don't?"

He squirmed a bit on the futon. "Naw. I don't think she's all that mysterious. She's just half-crazy, that's all."

"Crazy how?"

"You know that Thurber story, 'The Secret Life of Walter Mitty?'"

"Yeah . . . the Danny Kaye film."

He shook a battered Camel out of a soft pack and lit it clumsily from a book of matches. "She's like that. She thinks she's living this storybook fantastical life or some shit, but it's all in her fucked-up little head." He tapped the side of his head with an index finger.

"Well." I lit a smoke of my own. Our twin strands of sidestream played with each other up near the ceiling. "Tell me about the collaboration."

"It wasn't much of one, really. The idea was that I'd do base coats, like backgrounds, and then she'd paint figures, and after, I'd do glazes. I'm good with glaze."

"And?"

He tapped an ash angrily. "It was bullshit. I could do reds, blues—didn't matter. Her figures were all the same. She was always painting this one guy—" He broke off, staring intensely at me suddenly. "Wait a minute . . . you're the guy, aren't you? You know Ash already. What's this about?"

I shook my head and grinned as sincerely as I could. "I promise you, it's coincidence. Actually, I got hired to research her because the journalist writing the piece thought the same thing. Really, we've never met. I've never sat for her. I don't know a damn thing about art."

He blinked but bought it. "Weird. Well, that was the thing. It wasn't a collaboration because her part of it was always the same shit. I kept telling her she was crazy, that she couldn't get hung up on one subject. And, yeah, she never had a model that I knew of. I figured she just dreamed the guy up. But she always said, *He's real, I know he's real.* Weird dream-life nonsense. Fucking Walter Mitty."

"So she had an imaginary friend."

"No, that's the thing. She used to say that her paintings were important. *These are going to save him, wooo,*" he made a faux-spooky sound and waved his hands at me.

"Like her shit is so much more relevant because she's on some kind of mission, like a spy or something. She said the paintings could save her too. Get her out of her crazy life. Save her from an *untimely death*." He laughed, a bitter, rancid chuckle. "*An untimely death*. She said that all the time, like people were after her, jealous of her talent or something. Like she was too good to live. Drove me nuts so I called it all off. Three months working together, and I got nothing to show for it."

"But you think she's good, obviously."

"Well, yeah, she can paint. And she really watched people—used it in her work. But what's the use of painting if it's just the same thing over and over again, like that dude in New Orleans always painting that blue dog—I mean, what's the point? . . . I gotta piss."

As soon as he was out of the room I went to the shelf and picked up the photograph he had evidently tipped over. It was him, next to a pool, shirtless with a broad grin across his face, one arm holding a girl close to him. It was Ashley, I was sure of it. She was the right height, with jet-black hair, just to her shoulders, and a shy smile that played with itself upon the most lovely face I'd ever seen in my life. Aqualine features, skin pale without being pasty, knowing, heavy-lidded green eyes, sharp nose, and defiant chin. Gorgeous. She was wearing a yellow bikini top and her collarbone was exquisite. I heard Masello coming out of the bathroom but I let him catch me.

"Hey—"

I just looked at him. "What else, Masello?"

"Look, I don't know who you think you are—"

"Consider, just for a moment, that all that crazy stuff

going around in her head wasn't just her imagination. What if she were in some kind of trouble, and what if you were in a position to help her?"

"I don't need this kind of shit."

"Neither do I. But I'm not working on a story about her, and that's all I'm telling you because two people are dead already. What else, Masello?"

His cigarette was still smoking itself in the ashtray and he sat down heavily and picked it up. "All right. We were lovers first. I mean, that's how we decided to try to work together. I met her randomly, at the Pearl Paint on Market. She was just so hot, you know? I mean look at her, she's a knockout. Crazy as hell, I knew it right away, but crazy chicks are great in the sack, right?"

I just nodded to keep him talking.

"So we hooked up, and that was nuts, but she was fun in a kooky kind of way, and then we started working together. But she was worse as a lover than she was to work with. I mean this guy, the guy who looks like you, whoever he is—she's obsessed with him. She said that she was meant to be with him, that she was waiting for him, and that when the time was right . . ." He fell off and stamped out the smoke. "I mean, there's only so much of that you can listen to before you, you know."

"Kind of works against your self-esteem."

"Yeah. Totally. Like she's fucking you but she's thinking of someone else. Too weird. So I cut it off—the collaboration, the . . . everything."

"What about her family? You ever meet them?"

"Naw, wasn't much. Her mother's dead and she didn't know her father. I heard she lived in squats for a while, but she didn't like to talk about it. She had this uncle who was never around. I never met him, but I think he helped her with some bills."

"How did her mother die?"

"Lung cancer. After they moved up here from LA. You know—she grew up in fucking Anaheim. Disneyland, man. Her mom even worked there. That's where all that fantasy-land bullshit starts. Fucking Walt Disney. Those stories *fuck up* young girls."

"When was the last time you saw her?"

"Haven't talked to her in months. Then I heard she was gone."

"Heard how?"

"My girlfriend heard it from the guy at Pearl, at the paint counter. My girlfriend's an artist too. Ash had an account there. For years she kept a running tab, then one day she came in and paid it all off, real dramatic-like, classic Ash, and said she wouldn't come back. And she hasn't. I ask when I go in—she paints all the time, so that place is like her grocery store. If she's not shopping there she must've left town."

"How long ago was this?"

"Few weeks maybe? Not so long, but it's still fucking weird. I just hope I didn't have anything to do with it."

Vanity. "You didn't. I can almost promise you that."

"So, yeah, I just keep that picture to remind me. Just, you know . . . I hope she's okay. Coz she's a good person, just . . . a little crazy."

"What's the name of the guy at Pearl Paint?"

"I don't know, but he's always there. You can't miss him—looks just like Elvis Costello."

I chewed it over and decided to tell him: "Listen,

Jason, I'm hoping to prove that it isn't true, but there's a chance that Ashley . . . is already dead."

He burst out laughing. "Of course she's dead!" He kept laughing, and actually slapped his knee. "Yeah, she's dead, man! That's why she's gonna be so successful as an artist!"

I just looked at him.

"You don't know?"

Clearly I didn't.

"It's that old thing of how artists are never recognized in their own lifetime. But she had an ace in the hole, because she's already dead."

"What are you talking about?"

"*Keystroke error*, she called it," he said. "The Death Master File."

My face was blank.

"Social Security," he said. "They keep a list of everyone who's dead. The Death Master File. If you don't get reported dead, someone else can keep cashing your retirement checks or whatever. But if you *do* get reported dead, because some dumb clerk puts in the wrong Social Security number, then *bang*, you're dead. Your bank account is closed, you lose your house, whatever."

"This happened to Ashley?"

"Yeah." He stopped smiling. "I make fun of it, because it's just so Ash, you know? But it did kinda suck. She got on that list when she was barely eighteen, so she couldn't get off of it. She didn't have a paper trail, you know? She couldn't get a job unless it was under the table."

I stood up to put the photo back in its place, looking one more time at her devastating face. I would recognize it when I saw it again, and I would be seeing it in my dreams for a long time to come.

"It's crazy, man," Masello said. "Look into it. The Death Master File. Cool name for a band."

I sat down again. "Okay, Jason, here's the deal. I'm going to walk out of here and I'm never coming back. And I'm taking this," I picked my card up off the table, "with me. You won't see me again. You're a nice guy, and knowing me is really not a good idea right now. So one last thing: I have to find Ashley, and soon. So if there's anything else you know, anything at all that can help me find her, you have to tell me now."

He scratched his head quickly and fiercely, like a dog after a vigorous flea. "There's one place. A special place for her, that she goes to sometimes. If she's still in San Francisco, she'll go there sooner or later."

"Where?"

"Chinatown. Corner of . . . Washington and Grant. Some cheezy restaurant—Green Emerald? Emerald Princess? Something like that. You can't miss it—the downstairs is a junk tourist store, with a big spiral staircase with a big spiral Chinese dragon in the middle of it. You take the elevator up to the top floor and there's a restaurant, and a little cocktail lounge with big windows. You can see both bridges on a clear day. She took me there once. She loved it. Would just sit there for hours and stare."

"You haven't looked for her?"

"Naw. I got a new girlfriend now. I don't really want to see Ash again. She drives me nuts. I just hope she's okay."

"*Hellooooo!*" It was a muted, weirdly distorted call,

coming from the ancient intercom tube at the front door. Then the front door buzzer went off.

"That's my girl." He jumped up. "I thought you were her, actually. Little afternoon delight."

He yelled into the tube, "I'll be right down!"

I followed him into the stairwell and caught him by the arm. "If anyone else comes to you asking about Ashley, anyone that you don't know, you don't know her, you don't know anything. Knowing her could get you hurt."

"You're starting to sound just like her, man."

I followed him down the stairs where a plump blonde was waiting, wearing glasses with the geeky black-plastic birth-control frames that had inexplicably come into fashion forty years after never having been fashionable in the first place.

"Oh," she said when Masello opened the door, "I didn't know you had—"

"I'm on my way out," I said.

She offered me a hand and a genuine smile. "You are . . . ?"

"I'm nobody." I gave Masello a quick handshake. "I was never even here. Thanks."

"Right on. Good luck, man."

I went down the hill without looking back. Considering that I had learned about Masello from Dalton's notes, considering that Dalton was dead, considering that Susan had obtained the notes, undisturbed, from Dalton's apartment, considering that Susan was dead—I hoped that no other players would find Masello and he would live to create more bad art.

11

I was hungry. I took in the air and walked back down to Mission, cut up to 19th, and ducked into Cancún, the best damn taqueria in the city. The place was jumping, as usual, the long wooden tables crowded with strangers peeling the tinfoil from their monstrous burritos, bad salsa music blaring from speakers with blown woofers.

"*Hola*, Hernando."

"Hey, Da-veed, *qué pasa?* Long time no see." I'd helped his sister with a green card years ago and he always remembered me.

"Been busy."

"Better than dead."

"You?"

"*Mucho trabajo*, every day. Whatcha need?"

I ordered a super chicken and a horchata, grabbed a tray of chips with spicy green salsa, and wedged into a table next to a pretty girl who had a Chihuahua in the bag over her shoulder. She never looked at it, just ate her burrito; the dog looked up at me as if I were furniture. My number was called and I bit into a hot tortilla majestically wrapped around a perfectly balanced mixture of grilled chicken, black beans, Monterrey Jack cheese, guacamole, sour cream, and pico de gallo. Best lunch in town, and still under five bucks.

Something about the way the little dog looked at me reminded me of Dalton; the way he'd flinched when Sharkskin appeared in his doorway, like a dog being scolded. Then he'd composed himself and ushered me out, as if he knew what was coming and had accepted it. It was stupid to fixate on it, but with Dalton on my mind I looked around the room, eyeballing my fellow diners, especially the table near the door that was full of Mexican construction workers. Sharkskin looked nothing like these small, dark Sonorans. Maybe he was Spanish.

I finished up and tossed my trash. The place had thinned out a bit, and Hernando was leaning on the counter, almost imperceptibly moving his lips, singing along to the radio.

"Hey, Hernando. How can you tell if a guy is Spanish or just a light-skinned Mexican?"

He grinned. "You got a joke for me?"

"No, no," I said, laughing. "I met this guy and I can't figure out where he's from. It's driving me crazy."

He shrugged. "Hard to tell just by looking. Most Mexicans have some Spanish blood. What did he sound like?"

"I didn't hear him speak any Spanish."

"What about his English? *Deed hee talk like thees?*"

"Not at all. Just a slight accent, heavy on the *h*'s and *r*'s."

"Show me."

I'd only heard Sharkskin say a single sentence, but I remembered it exactly. I did my best, trying to hit the right spots, trying not to sound Jewish or like Peter Lorre. "I didn't *r*healize you *c*had a visit*urr*, Mr. Dalton. So *surrh*y to int*urrh*upt."

Hernando nodded, a tiny head bob becoming a vehement shake. "I know this guy. And I know why you don't." He turned and yelled toward the back of the kitchen: *"Oye, Pablito, ven aquí!"*

A short, skinny teenager in rubber gloves came out—the dishwasher. *"Repita para mi amigo en inglés."* He pointed at me. "Say it again, David." I did.

The kid looked up at me vacantly and, without emotion, said, "I didn't realize you had a visitor, Mr. Dalton. So sorry to interrupt." It was spooky. It was almost exactly as I'd heard it that day in the gallery, only more exaggerated. Sharkskin spoke better English than this kid, but they were from the same part of the world.

Hernando dismissed his young charge. *"Entonces?"*

"That was it. That was dead on."

"You're way off. Your friend isn't Spanish. He's Guatemalan."

I retrieved my car and drove west, preoccupied, and when I found myself on the tail end of Market I decided, for no good reason, to take a detour up to Twin Peaks. The road snaked around, climbing steadily upward, finally reaching the park with impeccable views. I parked and walked up the hill to take a look.

It was a clear day, the sky as blue as true optimism, the City laid out for me in all its splendor, nestled comfortably into the bay, looking calm and innocent from such a remove. I tried to pick out the *Chronicle* building at 5th and Mission, my old downtown stomping grounds, remembering a different time, full of deadlines and carpal tunnel syndrome and hurried lunches at Tu Lan, that fantastic pho joint around the corner on 6th, late nights stumbling out of the office, walking up Nob Hill to that great apartment I can't believe I ever gave up. From such a vantage, it was almost impossible to imagine the street view, the hard pavement, the tilting asphalt . . . like looking back in time.

The Golden Gate loomed in the distance, a testament to ingenuity and basic human stubbornness, the Marin Headlands a gloriously green backdrop. I remembered my last serious girlfriend—the last time I had a steady on the hook—and the night we drove over the bridge and parked at the lookout, with magnificent views of the City sparkling over the bay, got into the backseat and got right into it, top down and everything. She was sitting on top of me when another car parked beside us—teenagers, girls, who actually apologized for "intruding." Better times, before the alcoholism began to take its crippling toll, when I still fantasized about winning a Pulitzer, when Herb Caen was still alive and kicking, on the page and off, before he died and I wasn't even invited to the wake, all my bridges burned behind me. A bountiful civilization perched on a peninsula, jutting into a crystalline-blue halo, banked by beauty on all sides . . . a frontiersman's fantasy come to life. God's country, my grandmother used to call California. God's country.

And the death of Susan Dalton hanging over it all, a bleak shadow of uncertainty and menace.

I grabbed the painting from the trunk, left my car, and walked down the hill, letting the panorama vanish as I slowly descended to the level of the beaten and the miscreants. The steep hill dropped me onto Twin Peaks Boulevard, and I followed it around to Portola, making my way down into West Portal. I always liked this neighborhood, felt it would have suited my personality better than Nob Hill—or South City. Snuggled in between the mansion-riddled Forest Hill and St. Francis Wood, the neighborhood still has an unpretentious look and feel, with low buildings, a true "main street" with real shops, not chains, and residences lined up like soldiers, painted in muted tones. Not as cookie-cutter as Daly City, and not as far away as South City; peninsula living, but a short Muni ride away from downtown.

I found the art restoration shop and walked into a small receiving room with reproductions of famous works on the walls—Rembrandt, Caravaggio, Vermeer—along with a few modern oil paintings by unknowns. The door gave a little jingle as it closed behind me and a small but clear voice rang out from the back—"I'll be right with you!" I took a closer look at one of the oils on the wall, leaning in and allowing myself to be slightly mesmerized by the topography of the brushstrokes.

"How can I help you? . . . Oh, Mr. Crane! Nice to see you again."

"Katie, right? And it's David."

She was textbook: small and rather plain, with medium-length dark hair pulled back in a pragmatic ponytail and librarian glasses, wearing the obligatory hooded sweatshirt half-zipped over a baggy T. She was more tomboy than butch, cute with absolutely no effort, someone totally invested in a parallel world with little reason to pay attention to much else, and her eyes sparkled with a piercing intelligence. She had helped me research an artist for a potential buyer when she was still in grad school.

"David. Hi." She gave me a wry grin. "So, did your buyer ever make a decision?"

"He went another way. But I still got paid."

She gestured to my package. "What have you got?"

"This one is a little different." I put my package on the counter and peeled off the tarp, and she helped me unroll the canvas with small, well-worn hands. She smoothed it out and leaned her head back and to the side to take it in.

"It's fantastic."

"Uh . . . thanks. It's not mine, of course."

"Well, whoever did it, it's very good. What's wrong with it?"

"What?"

She laughed only slightly. "It doesn't seem to be in need of any repair. If you want it framed, I can recommend—"

"No, no. I want you to . . . tell me about it."

"What do you want to know?" She gave me a look of such simple curiosity that I almost didn't know how to answer.

What *didn't* I want to know? "The artist is a bit of a mystery . . . I don't know who she is, I barely know anything about her, and I have someone who wants to buy more of her work. I'm hoping there might be some clue in the painting as to who she is, maybe even how she can be found."

She nodded slowly. "Okay."

"I know it sounds crazy, but from what I've heard about the artist, she's a little . . ." I put out one hand, fingers spread, and waggled it unsteadily. "I think there might be something hidden in this painting. Maybe something in the materials—I don't know."

"I can analyze it, tell you about the paint, the canvas." She shrugged her shoulders. "If there is actually something hidden beneath the paint . . . I'd have to take it to the conservation laboratory at the Fine Arts Museum."

"Can you do that?"

"Sure. They have a spectrometer, X-ray . . . we use their facilities from time to time, but it's expensive, and it's not likely that I'll find anything."

"I don't care about the cost. I really want to know everything—anything you can tell me."

She smiled, and made a cracking noise out of the corner of her mouth. "I'll need a couple of days."

I wanted to think; I didn't want to think anymore. Susan Dalton kept swimming laps in the pool in my head, and some Guatemalan was playing lifeguard. The Pearl Paint lead was likely a dead end; it could wait. I needed something like a full-body yawn just to get my soul screwed on straight.

I walked back up to Twin Peaks, grabbed my car, rolled all the way down to Pier 39, and paid too much for parking. I spent a couple of hours leaning on the wooden railing, watching the sea lions sunbathing on the docks off the pier, listening to the bulls bray. It wasn't quite enough to drown it all out.

12

I woke up early, fried some eggs, and took a long, hot shower, thinking about the Death Master File. I knew a young computer wizard named Sobczyk I could ask about it—this shit was right up his alley—but he knew everything about everything; he'd talk my ear off.

I got dressed and dug into the Internet. Masello was on the level. There really is such a file, named like something out of a pulp novel or a *Star Wars* sequel, and they really do make mistakes.

On one hand, the money the government and corporations—mostly banks and insurance companies—lose by paying out millions in benefits to people who are already dead is a real problem. The actual reporting of the dead varies so widely from state to state that not everyone makes it into the Death Master File, or DMF, due to con-artistry or straight-up stupidity.

On the other hand, a simple human error in the data entry of a Social Security number can make a living person dead on paper. "Keystroke error." The error rate is tiny, between a third and a half of one percent. But 2.3 million people died in the US last year, which means that in 1996 alone, it's fair to assume that at least seven thousand people were declared dead but are still walking around dealing with it. You lose your house, you lose your bank account. You lose your pension, your health benefits—of course you lose your Social Security. And since Social Security sells the list to creditors and debtors, the damage is done even if you get yourself resurrected at the DMF level. Your death has trickled down the chain of information. Good luck convincing your bank that they should give you your money back.

I read a horror story about a woman who lived in her car for a while and spent five years trying to get herself declared legally alive, then I shut off the machine. Ash was unlucky, sure, but she was a scrapper. And I would find her.

I decided not to drive—it's impossible to park in Chinatown—so I walked down to the bus, rode to the BART, picked up and skimmed discarded newspapers on the train, got out at Montgomery, and hiked up the steep hill. Grant. Chinatown . . . tourists strolling and junk stores blaring crappy noise-making toys, with incense and fireworks and *San Francisco*-emblazoned everything. I've always liked Chinatown—the Chinese locals shoving tourists out of the way, the allure of cheap dumplings, a hanging duck through a dirty window, the crackle of Cantonese.

I found the place easily, right where Masello said it would be, even if he didn't know the name: The Empress of China. The downstairs was, indeed, a junk shop, with a spiral staircase and a Chinese dragon suspended inside its curve, mimicking the helix. I took the elevator to the sixth floor and walked out into the restaurant. I was standing in a small, almost circular foyer, decked out to look like the inside of a pagoda, and to my right was the dining room. To my left was the cocktail lounge, two sides of which were tall windows that offered views overlooking Chinatown. One wall separated the lounge from the restaurant, and was backed by the bar. The fourth wall, the short one to my left as I entered the lounge, was decorated with something that seemed shockingly out of place in a Chinese restaurant: a portrait of me.

It was less a portrait than a film still. I was bent over a woman, holding myself up with one arm while my other hand caressed her cheek. I knew the woman, of course; it was a recent lover, maybe a year ago—it didn't last more than a couple months. We were in my bed together, visible only from the waist up, where the covering of the blankets began and the edge of the canvas soon ended. We were illuminated from the side by a candle that flickered ghostly at the edge of the frame. Her eyes were closed and her mouth half open in apparent bliss. Her face was barely an impression, almost unfinished; she was buried under my body, except for one exposed breast shamelessly facing the viewer. My eyes were wide open, staring at the face underneath me, harsh with intention. The light across my body was golden, majestic, making me look almost holy. The brushstrokes were lovingly applied, if there is such a thing, as if the artist were touching my body tenderly with every stroke, anointing my eyes with somber blessing, caressing my face more intensely and successfully than I could caress the face of my lover. It was as if she were there, as if the artist were in the room with us, like a slightly jealous voyeur, happy to be watching but would be happier to be beneath me. It was too much. I had to turn away.

And when I did, I was looking right into the face of an older, lovely Chinese woman, wearing a tight dress with a Mandarin collar and off-center frogs, smiling and handing me a folded beverage napkin.

I took it without a word, ready for anything. I opened it up and there again, in that tender handwriting, was a short message: *Someday we'll sit here together. Have a plum wine. Look at the view. It's lovely.*

It was, and the plum wine was delicious. I sat at a low-lying table, right up at the edge of the enormous windows, looking out over Chinatown and North Beach, the bay beautiful and glaring, the Golden Gate just hidden in a shroud of lingering fog, and the Bay Bridge barely visible in the distance. Leaning over, I could clearly see the decorative Chinatown streetlight, dragon and all, just in front of the Kowloon Restaurant at the far corner of Grant and Washington.

I was dazed. There was something definitively unnerving about trying to find a woman who knew where I would be before I did. The waitress could only tell me that Ashley used to come and sit for hours, staring out at the view and drinking plum wine, but they never spoke other than customer-waitress niceties. Ashley's last visit had been a few weeks ago, when she asked the waitress for a favor and left the note—and the painting—for me.

I stepped up for a closer look and checked the date in the corner: *11/15/96.* Once again, that would be about right. Another snapshot from my life. I removed the painting from the wall and took it out with me. It was beautiful. It made me want to meet the woman who had painted it, to touch the hands that had touched the brush that touched this canvas. To look into the eyes that had seen this scene and seen only love.

I had to get the new evidence off to Katie. I half-ran down to the Montgomery station, jumped on the Muni, and rode under Market, popping out at street level at West Portal.

When I arrived at her shop I opened the door so fast I almost broke it. Katie was at the front counter with a phone in her hands.

"David, are you okay? I was just trying to call you."

"I have another painting." The door closed behind me and I caught my breath and my demeanor. "I'm . . . sorry. It's been a crazy day already."

"Tell me about it. You should . . ." She caught a look at the painting in my hands. "They are paintings of you, aren't they? I didn't want to say anything yesterday, but—"

"Honestly, I think the less you know about this, the better. I don't have any good answers anyway."

She nodded. "Come on back. I have to show you something."

Every wall of the back room was covered in bookshelves, and every available shelf was stacked with art books. A series of large tables held different canvases in various states of restoration. Mine was laid out flat.

"This is your basic late twentieth-century oil-on-canvas painting," she explained. "The canvas is nothing special, basically the kind of thing you buy prestretched at any art supply store. The oil is the same—standard, run-of-the-mill oil paint. It's in excellent condition, and I'd say that the date at the bottom is probably accurate—

this painting was definitely completed within the last year. Either way, it's not special."

"So you didn't find anything out of the ordinary?"

"Not at first. But I went down to the Fine Arts Museum this morning, just to have a look. You said you wanted to know about anything . . . hidden. When I looked with a better pair of eyes, I did find something."

She flipped on a photographer's light box and slid an X-ray onto it. "This," she said, pointing to an oblong shape toward the top right corner of the painting, maybe two inches by a half-inch. It jumped out of the otherwise unvaried X-ray—something totally different than the rest of the painting.

"What is it?"

"I'm not sure. At first it reminded me of a Chinese seal—you know, a signature stamp, as if the artist had used a stamp to mark the signature, or maybe the studio. It would almost make sense, since there's no signature on the painting." She shook her head. "But that's just my brain thinking aesthetically. This is so visible in the X-ray . . . it has to be something foreign, something buried beneath layers of paint. Whatever it is, it's an addition—it's not paint, and it's not part of the canvas. Perhaps the artist used some sort of found object as part of the composition, and then later decided against it and painted over it rather than going through the trouble of removing it. Judging by the density, it could be plastic, or a light metal. But it almost looks like a computer chip." She was right. If you really squinted, you could see intricate traces that could be some kind of circuitry.

"Can you take it out?"

She made a face. "I can't promise you that I won't

damage the painting. I'd have to lift the top layers of paint away—it's a beautiful portrait, David. I could ruin it at worst, or at best decrease its value."

"Do it."

She nodded and flipped the lights on and moved to her worktable, selecting a few sharp stainless-steel instruments like a dental hygienist at a cleaning. She worked at the painting with surgical precision, positioning a goose-neck lamp over the area in question, gently making incisions and lifting layers of paint. After only a few minutes she had worked her way under the foreign object and suddenly gasped.

"What is it?"

"I—I don't know. But . . . look." She lifted with a small, flat knife. "It just comes right off." She was holding a small, thin rectangle of paint, and the place she had removed it from looked almost exactly the same.

"It was meant to be removed?"

"It would appear that way. You can't even tell anything's been taken out."

It was true. Apart from a slight unevenness in the thickness of the paint, the image was unaltered. She handed me the object. It looked like aluminum, but was encased in a rubbery sheath. One end slipped right off, revealing a USB plug. It was some kind of computer gadget.

"That's really weird," Katie said. "Maybe it was an accident."

"Let's find out." I grabbed the Chinatown painting and put it on the table.

Katie swung her lamp around, blasting the painting as if it were under interrogation, and squatted down to look at the topography of the canvas from eye level. It didn't take more than a minute. "Yes, right here. Top right corner again. Once you know what you're looking for, it's easy. The paint is just a little too thick, compositionally." She looked up at me, blinking rapidly. "Should I?"

I nodded.

In moments she handed me another object, the same exact thing as the first.

"This is really weird, David. I don't know what—"

"Exactly. You don't know. And I think that's best. I'm paying you in cash, and I'll throw in a little extra. I was never here, understand?"

"Are you . . . in some kind of trouble?"

"I don't know. But I want to make sure you're not. Just forget all about this." I pocketed the devices, knowing where my next stop would be. "Listen, I've got like twelve other errands to run today. Can you just ship the paintings back to me? No rush."

"Of course."

Katie stopped me on my way out. "If you do get to the bottom of all this, dude, come by. I'd like to hear about it."

"I'll do that."

13

"All right, all right, I'm comin'."

I didn't stop banging on the door.

"All RIGHT already."

The house was a big Victorian facing Alamo Square—a much nicer place than one would expect guys like these to live in, but they'd been renting the top floor for years. A typical San Francisco arrangement—an older lesbian couple had the main floor, a straight couple had the lower apartment, and two weird computer freaks and their machines occupied the four bedrooms of the top floor. I turned toward the park to admire the view, then finally heard soft, quick footsteps coming down the stairs. That would be Rider. The door opened, and Rider stuck his head out and blinked behind his wire-rimmed glasses.

"Holy shit! Itchy Crane!" He lurched out, a tall, gangly piece of work, and gave me a bear hug.

"Ooph," I mocked. "You been working out?"

"Yeah, yeah, I have," he said, without a trace of guile. "Thanks for noticing. Come in, come in, Sobczyk will be hella psyched to see you."

I followed him up the stairs. Rider and Sobczyk had both worked in the IT department at the *Chronicle* at one time or another, though they generally made more money freelancing. They were geeks, good guys, albeit a little crackers. Rider was from Kansas, and had moved to San Jose straight out of high school and worked for a series of Silicon Valley firms before relocating to the City. He was quick, fairly social for his type, and with a last name like Rider no one ever used his first name. Sobczyk had a similar affliction—he looked 100 percent Chinese, and you'd never guess his father was Polish if it weren't for the last name. He was a native San Franciscan, heavyset, moody, paranoid, and a genius. They were both incredibly young.

I'd been to the house a dozen times and still couldn't figure out where either of them slept—every room was a labyrinth of computers, hardware, and textbooks. The two of them seemed to wander from room to room, each taking turns lending his particular skills to various projects. I often wondered if they slept at all. We found Sobczyk in the kitchen, the one room that was always immaculate, intensely focused on moving a toasted peanut butter and jelly sandwich from a wooden cutting board to a plate. He didn't glance over when we came in.

"Sobczyk—check it out, it's Itchy Crane," Rider announced.

Sobczyk looked up at me, gave the slightest of smiles from the corners of his mouth, gently raised his eyebrows—twice—and took a bite out of his sandwich.

"Told you he'd be psyched," Rider said. "I haven't see him this excited since we beat that virus last month for Skywalker. Come on in—lay it on me." I followed him into one of the rooms and he cleared a stack of books from a piano bench so that I could sit next to his wheeled office chair, which was pulled up to a desk with exactly enough free space on it to harbor a keyboard and a flat-screen monitor. As soon as his ass hit the chair he began clicking into several different windows at once, working the mouse which was set on a doorstop of a technical manual ramped at a forty-five-degree angle to the desk. "Go ahead, talk to me, I just gotta finish this one thing." You had to focus to talk to Rider—he was deftly capable of doing six things at once, and it was difficult to keep track of your own thoughts without being distracted by his activity.

"I'm into some shit, Rider. Some bad shit. So I just want to say, first thing"—I heard a crunch behind me, and realized Sobczyk had come in with his sandwich—"to both of you. I was not here today. And anything I show you, anything I tell you, you can't tell anybody."

"Ooo, sounds spooky." Rider's hands came off the keyboard just long enough for him to wiggle his fingers like a villain from a *Scooby-Doo* cartoon.

"No bullshit. I need you to promise."

"Of course, Itchy. You know we work on top secret shit all the time. You can trust us."

"Okay. What is this?" I tossed one of the strange devices from Ashley's paintings onto Rider's keyboard. He actually stopped working.

"Where did you get that?" Sobczyk asked. He put down his sandwich.

Instead of answering, I handed Sobczyk the other device. The two of them turned the devices around in their hands.

"It's so beautiful," Sobczyk said.

"Totally . . . it's even cooler than I thought it would be."

"Where did you get these?" Sobczyk asked again.

"Wouldn't help if I told you. What are they?"

"I can't fucking believe you have these!" Rider almost yelled. "Holy crap, these aren't even supposed to exist yet! I heard these wouldn't come out until . . . like, 2000 or something."

"They've been working on them in Singapore," Sobczyk added. "But . . . what he said."

"What is it? And please remember I'm not a computer guy—I just want to know what it is and what it's used for."

"It's a flash memory storage device," Rider said. "It's for storing shit, just like a floppy disk."

"So what's so cool about it?"

"Well . . . they're not out yet. No one's seen 'em—it's like this crazy rumor that we'll have these in a couple of years—and you have *two* of them. These must have come from somewhere on high, or from someone with some serious connections."

"That's why we think they're cool," Sobczyk chimed in, "but everyone will think so if they ever get released. See, a floppy disk only holds two megabytes of information—1.44, for all intents and purposes. The promise of the flash drive is that it can hold more data. Much more."

"Data storage. Okay. So what's on it?"

Rider's eyes went wild with excitement. "Let's find out!" He plugged the USB into his machine and started clicking the mouse. "That's the other cool thing. These are supposed to pop right up, none of that grinding, waiting around like with floppies—see? It's there already." He opened a window. "Holy crap!"

"I don't believe it," Sobczyk said.

"What is it?"

Rider leveled his gaze at me and dropped his voice. "It's eight megabytes. That's like five floppy disks!"

"I don't believe it," Sobczyk said again.

"I know we're all very excited here, but I need to know what's on it."

"Just give me a few minutes," Rider said.

I got up and Sobczyk picked up his plate. "You want a sandwich?" he asked.

"Love one."

Watching Sobczyk make a peanut butter and jelly sandwich was an exercise in Zen. He was so serious, so methodical, he took a mundane sandwich and raised it to a level of high art. It was clear that he found the act deeply relaxing.

"Sobczyk," I said, as he stood over his toaster watching the bread like a mama bird. I hesitated. He'd give me the full Funk & Wagnalls, but I needed to know, and Sobczyk would know.

"Yes?"

"What do you know about Guatemala?"

"A little," he said. "In terms of what?"

"In terms of a guy from Guatemala who might be a killer."

"No news there," he said. "Guatemala has been in the midst of a civil war for thirty, thirty-five years. A lot of Guatemalans are killers."

"A thirty-five-year civil war?"

"You don't read the paper much, do you?" He shrugged. "Wouldn't matter. They don't print much about it in American papers, since the whole thing is basically our fault."

It was impossible to get cranky with a guy for acting

superior when his knowledge was, beyond a doubt, superior. "Tell me about it."

"You ever heard of United Fruit?"

"No."

"It's bananas."

"Crazy?"

"No. Bananas. It all started with bananas. A couple hundred years ago, no one in the States had ever seen a banana. Within a century, they started to sell like—well, bananas. So a company in Boston goes into business with a railroad entrepreneur and they form United Fruit, which buys up a bunch of land in Guatemala and corners the market. Send bananas to the coast by rail, ship them to the States, make a ton of money. Everything is great for fifty years." The toaster popped and Sobczyk took out the bread and laid it on a cutting board. He opened a jar of peanut butter and rummaged in a drawer for a butter knife.

"In 1951, Jacobo Árbenz gets elected president of Guatemala—arguably, the most democratically elected president to date. But he's progressive. He realizes that the biggest landowner in his country is a foreign corporation, and it doesn't pay any taxes. So Árbenz decides he's going to expropriate land from United Fruit and give it back to the indigenous population so they can farm their own land. Rich white men don't like this." He was drawing the peanut butter across the bread in long, even strokes, leaving a nice striation from the serrated edge of the knife.

"United Fruit's lobbyists start talking to Washington. They tell everyone that Árbenz has communist seats in his congress—which was true, but it was a tiny minority. No big deal. But it's the fifties, people are freaked out, and Secretary of State John Dulles and his brother Allen—the director of the CIA—convince Eisenhower that having communists so close to our borders is no good. The whole thing goes down Black Ops." He got a clean knife from the drawer and started in on the grape jelly, slathering it onto the clean slice of toast.

"It's 1953. The CIA handpicks Castillo Armas, an ex-iled fucking furniture salesman living in Honduras, to be the next president. They start a massive propaganda campaign, running a radio broadcast out of Honduras, flying over the capital and dropping flyers—calling for Árbenz to step down or be overthrown. Armas has an army of about two hundred other exiles, and they cross the Honduran border and camp out at the Church of the Black Christ in Esquipulas. There are a few skirmishes along the way, and Armas isn't doing that well, but the propaganda machine is making the army sound bigger than it is, and the international press is picking it up. It was a hoax of *War of the Worlds* proportions, with just enough reality thrown in to sell it. The CIA brings in pilots to strafe a couple towns, do some fly-bys, even blowing up some gas tanks at the Guatemala City airport." He tossed the two butter knives in the sink. "You don't want to know all this. I always do this—I'm way off topic."

"No, please. This is fascinating."

"Well, short version: The people are panicking, no one is backing Árbenz, the American ambassador is whispering in his ear . . . Árbenz abdicates the presidency to Armas, who gives United Fruit everything they want. Coups beget coups, it's one junta after another. Armas gets assassinated in '57. Anyway, the coup was so successful, the CIA thought they'd try it again in Cuba. Remember Bay of Pigs?" He didn't wait for an answer. "I could go on, but it's all death squads, assassinations . . . in the eighties it got even worse, what with the Reagan administration encouraging military leaders to fight insurgents. Something like a million people fled to Mexico and the US. If you didn't run fast enough, you were dead. Anyway, the point is, Guatemala has been basically fucked since the fifties. And it's all our fault." Sobczyk put the sandwich together, sliced it in half with a single downstroke of a carving knife, set it on a plate, and handed it to me.

"Did you see that thing, what, two years ago?" Sobczyk asked. "How they were finally asking questions about that American who got murdered?

"Can't say I did." I picked up a half and took a bite.

"Michael DeVine. Lived in Guatemala since the seventies, owned an inn with his wife. In 1990 they found him on his ranch with his hands tied and his head nearly cut off. They eventually convicted a military officer of the killing, but there was a colonel who was implicated as being involved. He never cooperated, he hindered the investigation—probably did some cover-up. Two years ago it comes out that he was a paid informant of the CIA. And he stayed on the CIA's payroll for two years after the DeVine murder. Paid by the CIA, and harboring death squads who are killing Americans. It was on *Charlie Rose*, man. I know it sounds unrelated, but you're asking about a Guatemalan killer? In the world of conspiracies, there's nothing more natural. This isn't ancient history. This is now."

"And the civil war?"

"Officially, it's over. The government and the gueril-
las signed a peace accord last December. We'll see how
that goes."

"Sobczyk," I said, "I have to admit, this is the best
PB&J I've ever eaten."

"Itchy." It was Rider, and he looked like he'd seen a
ghost. "You need to see this."

He brought a series of color photographs up on his
computer screen that appeared to be taken from a vantage point somewhere in the ceiling of my kitchen. They
were all of me, and each image had a time-and-date
stamp on the bottom. The date was 8/18/97—the same
date as on Ashley's painting—and the time began just
before noon and ended just after three in the afternoon.
Rider flipped from one image to the next, about two
dozen in total, telling the story of my afternoon that day:
my barber comes in, cuts my hair, and leaves. I spend
the next two hours making an idle lunch—soup and a
sandwich—and reading the paper. A typically boring
afternoon for me, and Ashley had picked the most interesting aspect to paint.

"Your house is wired," Sobczyk said.

"These are video stills," Rider said, "taken from a
security camera. You've got a camera in your kitchen."

"What about the other device?"

"These are . . ." Rider blushed, "even worse."

They had obviously come from the Chinatown painting. The images showed me and a woman having sex in
my bed. Rider flipped through them a little too slowly,
and said, "She's really—"

"All right."

He flipped ahead. The girl got dressed and left, and

I got up and sat at my desk drinking whiskey and smoking for another two hours. Again, Ashley had picked the best part. The date stamp was 11/15/96, same as on the painting.

"You have a camera in your bedroom," Sobczyk said.

"Someone's bugging you," Rider said. "Or at least was, when these were taken. You ever notice a big truck parked outside your house?"

"No, why?"

"Doesn't matter," Sobczyk said. "You don't have to be that close anymore. They could have a signal, bounce it off of satellites."

"Maybe, but that would have to be a powerful signal. What about a relay? To send it a few miles—"

"What are we talking about here?"

"The footage has to be collected somewhere," Rider explained. "If you have video cameras in your house, someone has to come in to collect the tapes. It's more likely that the tape is somewhere else—that the camera sends the data to another location to be recorded. Like in the movies—the FBI parked outside a mobster's house in a bread truck. A deer blind. Something right out in the open that you'd never notice. Sobczyk is just saying that, in theory, the bread truck could be anywhere. You'd have to take a look at the cameras—find them, crack them open, see what kind of transmitter they're using. We could totally do that for you. We could come over right now and—"

"Not a good idea, Rider. Not now, anyway. If these people are still watching me, I can't have them knowing that I know. I might take you up on that offer at a later date." I pulled out my wallet and peeled off a couple hundreds. "Here," I said. "Thanks for the help, both of you."

"Itchy, come on," Rider whined. "We don't want your money. This is fun—let us work with you."

"It's not fun, it's dangerous. Trust me on this one. If I can use you, I'll let you know. Can you burn this stuff onto a CD for me and keep a copy?"

"Already done." Rider handed me a CD.

"Don't show this stuff to anyone."

"Promise."

"I gotta go."

Sobczyk looked disappointed, and I slapped him on the shoulder. "Hey, Itchy," he said. "Just . . . you should check and see if your phones are tapped. Or if there's a bug in your car. Just . . . so you know."

"Thanks. I'll be in touch."

14

I went up the street and waited for the 21-Hayes, positively shaking. If nothing else, I finally understood how Ashley had managed to paint my portrait without my having sat for her. The real question was, why? Why was my house bugged in the first place? Tapped phones were one thing, but video cameras? In two rooms of the house—that I knew of? Who in the world would care so much about a floundering information broker to keep such close tabs? And why would a twenty-something artist have access to the footage? Why would she paint what she saw in these videos and then bury the film in the painting? And how would she have access to devices that weren't supposed to exist yet?

It drew into sharp relief the question of who was after what. Ashley was missing, Conrad didn't want me to find her, Conrad didn't want anyone to have these paintings, McCaffrey sent me a painting, McCaffrey wanted me to find Ashley—and her paintings were the only real clues. I remembered what Dalton had said to Ashley: *These paintings are to die for.* They're loaded, all right. I wondered if anyone, besides me, even knew what was hidden in the paintings.

I got on the bus, riding down toward Market. *Fuck Ashley,* I thought. *I want to know who's spying on me, even if I never find out why.* I found myself, once again, asking impossible questions about loyalty and motive—the eternal variables of a conspiracy. My best hunch, and my best bet, had to be Conrad, and I knew someone who could lead me to him.

I passed the porn shop on Market and wasn't surprised to see Alan Punihaole's beat-up Datsun parked just around the corner on Golden Gate. I went up the rickety back stairs of Hollywood Billiards and spotted him right away, swimming in a haze of smoke, shooting Nine-ball in the corner with a skinny black kid smoking those cheap Garcia y Vega cigarillos. When Al saw me coming he did a double take, got control of his bowels, chalked up his cue, and leaned in casually for a tough combo from the three to the nine. He missed.

"'Scuse me a minute," he said to the kid, and stepped aside. "What can I do for you, Mr. Crane?"

"I need to find Conrad. I want to know where he lives, where he eats, where he takes a shit."

"I tole you before, Mr. Crane, I don't know much."

"When you give him a ride somewhere, where do you pick him up?"

"Sometimes he meets me here, sometimes I get him across the street."

"Across the street?"

"The Market Street Cinema. He's sweet on a girl there—drops in almost every afternoon. He might be there now."

"Now why didn't you tell me that the last time we saw each other?"

"I was scared shitless, man! Don't you remember?"

"All right, all right." There was no use leaning on

him; it only raised his blood pressure. "When did you see him last?"

"Couple days ago. But he was just paying me for the last time. For, you know, visiting you."

"Any plans to see him again?"

"Later tonight."

"See, that's the kind of thing I want to know, Al."

"I'm sorry, Mr. Crane. You make me nervous."

The skinny black kid potted the nine and was coming around to shake Al's hand. "Nice game," he said, grinning. Al forced a half-smile that came out more like a grimace. I really did make him nervous.

"Come on," I said, putting my hand on his shoulder. "Let me buy you a drink." He needed to relax if he was ever going to be of any use to me.

Al sucked down half an imported beer in one gulp, put his foot on the rail and his ham hock of an arm on the bar, and seemed to settle down a little bit. I sipped my whiskey and took in the scene.

"How did you get mixed up with Conrad in the first place?"

Al finished his beer and I held out a finger to the bartender for another. "Thanks," Al said, looking down. He was downright bashful when you got him alone. He leaned in toward me. "I used to be really good, all right? All I did was hustle here, and I did pretty good."

"You mean pool?"

"I did good. But then these black guys started hanging out here, and—I ain't racist or nothin', but some of 'em are good, and my game started slipping a little."

"Because these guys are better than you?"

"Naw . . . I don't know. My mom got sick, I needed

money, there was more pressure . . . it used to be easier, you know, just make enough to pay rent, buy some beers. No pressure."

"You have to relax, Al. You can't win a pool game if you're worried about your mom."

"I know, I know." He hit his beer. "But when Conrad started coming around, I thought I could use the money. I'm not a criminal. I mean, hustling pool isn't exactly illegal."

I had to appreciate his slippery sense of morality, and wondered if I could exploit it. "So Al," I asked conspiratorially, "what kinds of things do you do for Conrad?"

"Not much, really," he said, his eyes going all shifty. "I took him to Oakland once, I helped him brace this one guy . . ." He trailed off, shifting his weight from side to side. "He's an okay guy, but I think he's into some weird stuff, and—I don't want to know. I just do what he asks and try to stay out of it. Drive the car. Look mean. That's it."

"Is it like a regular thing? If he doesn't drive—"

"No, man. I done maybe three or four jobs for him. Just in the last few months. I'm not like his chauffeur or nothing. He takes a lot of cabs. Just when he needs another pair of hands."

"So what's on for tonight?"

"See, after last time, after I got into so much trouble with you, you know?" I nodded. "I was kind of mad. Like, he shouldn't be getting me in trouble. So when he came by to pay me, I said that was too risky, and maybe he could throw me some other work. Easier work."

"Did you tell him I came to see you?"

"No," he replied, his eyes going wide. "This guy's

half crazy. He would kill us both." He finished his beer; I motioned the bartender over. "All I said is, *If you're gonna take cabs everywhere, you might as well use me for long trips*—save him some money, and I get paid."

"You're really strapped, huh?"

"It's my mom, I—you don't care about my problems."

Everyone has a sob story. "Don't worry, Al, you're a resourceful guy." It always came down to money, and it was nice to know that Al's loyalty was for sale. I threw some money on the bar for the drinks and peeled off a couple twenties for Al. "Take this, all right?"

"You said I owed you a favor."

"Yeah, but I'm asking a little more than a favor. I don't want to get you into trouble, but I might not be able to help it. Tell me more about tonight."

He eyed me nervously, then looked at the money on the bar. "I did this job for him once in Foster City. On the way back he stopped in San Mateo. Said he went to this place all the time. So I said to him, *Next time you go down there, I'll drive you.* It's an expensive cab ride."

"Where are you meeting him?"

"Here, sometime after ten. He's gonna call here when he's on his way over."

"Fine." I chewed it over. "I want you to call me after you hear from him. If it all goes smoothly, there's another fifty in it for you."

"If you're gonna tail us, don't drive. Conrad knows your car—he'll spot it in a second."

Al wasn't as dumb as he let on, but that didn't mean I could trust him. "Al, who says I'm gonna tail you? Listen, there's some weird shit going on, so trust me when I tell you I am not the only guy you have to worry about."

He looked so nervous I actually thought he would whimper. "Just don't say a word to Conrad, all right? I was never here."

"Never saw you."

"I'll be having drinks down the street at the 711 Club."

"I know it."

"Call me at the bar when you hear from him. Then forget about me."

"Okay."

I turned to leave.

"Mr. Crane?"

I looked back.

"What is this really all about?"

"Can't say I know, Al. I think the less you know, the better. Just watch your back." I was starting to like him.

15

I wanted some answers and couldn't think of any reason to stay below the radar—I *was* the radar. Might as well cross the street and give it a shot. Conrad could stand to be rattled a little.

It was twenty to get into the Market Street Cinema; the VIP room in back was extra.

The place did look like an old cinema—beat-up, semen-stained, flip-up theater seats with split wooden arm rests raked on a sticky black floor. There was a large stage in front where a completely nude, statuesque blonde was barely shaking herself to the overly loud heavy-metal music that came over the cracked PA. I spotted Conrad immediately, sitting down in front, eating pistachios and looking bored. This wasn't his girl.

I hadn't even made it halfway down the aisle when a trashy-looking tawny matron—well past her prime and with a bad boob job that was going south quick—asked me, "Would you like to come in back and get your penis serviced?" I couldn't imagine being in the mood.

I sat down next to him. He gazed at my shoes, obviously annoyed that I was sitting so close considering how empty the place was, but he didn't look at my face and didn't speak.

I broke the ice: "How are you this afternoon?"

"Fuck off," he rasped at me, still not looking. "If I want a blow job I'll pay for it in back."

"Well, hello to you too, Conrad."

He looked at me then. The recognition went across his face like a bright light in a darkened outhouse. He was happy to see me. "Well, if it isn't Itchy Crane. You should have made an appointment. If I knew you were coming to my office I would have put on a pot of coffee."

"You needn't bother. Pure coincidence, really. I'm hot on a slinky little brunette who's coming on in a minute."

"Oh, you still like little brunettes, do you?" He laughed a ghastly little laugh that was absent of mirth.

"You could say that."

"I thought we convinced you to get off that trip, Itchy. What, you thick-headed?"

"Oh, not at all. See, I already had it cracked before you came to see me."

"Really?"

"Really. She's working at a diner off the 5 up near Redding. You know, greasy eggs and undercooked home fries. Goes by the name of Gladys. Saving up for a sex change."

He looked at me stiffly. He'd have killed me just as easily. "You're funny." The blonde walked offstage to hustle lap dances. There was a minute to wait before the next girl.

"But what I can't figure is why you didn't ask me that in the first place. Why scare me off if you're looking for her yourself?"

"Who said I'm looking for anyone? Maybe I'm the one who disappeared her in the first place."

"Not buying it. You'd just let me look, knowing I wouldn't find anything."

Steely Dan's "Hey Nineteen" came on beneath an incoherent babble of introduction from the deejay. "Shut up," he said, "this is my girl."

I decided to let him enjoy it. She was a redhead, very young and innocent-looking, big boobs, cute, nothing special. Had to be a type thing. She did a soft, sauntering striptease to the Steely Dan, then disappeared behind the curtained doorway at the top of the stage while the deejay blabbered some more gibberish hype. She came back through the curtains fully naked, with a wide pudendum shaved into a scarlet landing strip, thrashing around suggestively to No Doubt's "Don't Speak." I watched Conrad watching her; he was enthralled, totally consumed. There was no room in his tiny Jurassic brain for anything else. He offered up a ten spot and she came over to do a little wiggle just for him. I held up a single and let her slap her boobs around in front of my face. When she was done she went back through the curtain, reappearing in the audience seconds later in a tight leopard-print outfit. She came straight to Conrad and gave him a chaste kiss on the cheek. "I'll be right with you, sweetheart," she whispered, and then looked at me. "Care for a private dance?"

"Not today, sweetheart," I responded, and she moved off to hustle the few other stragglers in the room.

"All right," he said finally. "You got about two minutes to speak your piece before I go in the back room."

"You killed Susan Dalton." I didn't think for a minute that he had, but I thought it would get the ball rolling.

"And what if I did?"

"You're next."

He laughed long and hard. When he stopped, he stopped suddenly and gave me a steady, snakelike gaze, one hand unconsciously crossing his chest. He was packing. "You want to step outside I'll be more than happy to put a bullet in you right now."

"You could have killed me back at my place if you wanted to."

"I would have if I been PAID to. But if you want to get smart I'll do it gratis."

"So why not knock me off from the get-go? Or don't the guys who do your thinking for you tell you that much?"

"You really want to know who killed Susan Dalton?"

"Yes, I do."

"Same guy who killed her brother, pal. You."

"Excuse me? That red bush go to your head, or—"

"Dumb-ass. You're pegged, buddy. They can put you at the scene of both crimes, and they got guns with your prints on 'em. You're still alive coz you're made to order—sliced, diced, and dressed. But by my thinking—what little I'm at liberty to do—it don't matter now at all. Dead or alive, you're still a steak dinner." He licked his lips with a narrow tongue. "If you'll excuse me, I have a date."

He got up and left me looking at a skinny brunette with track marks. I left before I had to see her naked. On my way up the raked auditorium I ran across the trashy matron who wanted to service my penis. "Hey, doll," I asked, "who was that cute redhead who just finished up?"

"Oh," she said, "that's Karyn, with a y. Sweet girl. Want to come back and meet her?"

"No thanks, I'll come back later."

She gave me a wink and an ass jiggle as she walked away.

I stumbled out onto Market with my head positively reeling. Conrad was an evil bastard, to be sure, and probably a killer for hire, but he didn't strike me as stupid. I found it hard to believe that he would lay something so heavy on me if it weren't at all true. Then again, if it was true, why tell me? What hard evidence could incriminate me in the Dalton deaths? My fingerprints weren't on record anywhere. No murder weapons were recovered, at least none that I knew of. I knew there was no weapon at the Dalton Gallery, and I couldn't imagine one had been left behind at Susan's.

I rode the BART to Colma—the end of the line—and got on the bus headed home. My head was still spinning. I felt like a drink, but I knew that if I had one it would mean ten more and I'd never figure anything out. Susan's death was hanging on me, and because Conrad's accusation had a little truth to it, I couldn't shake the feeling that she was dead because of me. I wondered how long I had left, and worse, what might happen to Masello, sweet Katie, even Rider and Sobczyk—anyone I'd seen in the last couple of days. Did anyone have long to live? Suddenly the thought of going home and walking around like a marionette before an unknown audience and with no knowledge of who was pulling the strings made me completely ill.

16

I figured I could get in just before closing and rode the bus all the way to the gun range. "Am I too late?" I asked Charlie.

She checked the clock. "Naw, you're fine. What are you into? Hey, I got this sweet Walther PPK 7.65—it's the James Bond gun."

"Just give me a .45, will you?"

"You didn't bring yours?"

"I haven't been home. But it's all I'm in the mood for."

"Got a Remington Rand right here. It'll feel just like yours."

I stepped onto the range and fired clip after clip. I kept sending the target out farther and farther, blasting at the silhouette with focused precision, feeling the power of the gun, the secure, heavy weight of it in my hand, the comfortable kick as the rounds left the barrel. I was at ease, in the perfect peace of vengeful meditation, imagining Susan's killer with every squeeze. Take aim, breathe, shoot him right through the heart. Aim, breathe, right between the eyes. Conrad, dead. Sharkskin, dead. Conrad's words were swirling: *You're pegged, buddy.* Prints on the gun. Why would he tell me? Aim. Breathe. Shoot. Prints on the gun. Aim. Breathe. Shoot. No gun at the crime scene. Gun with prints.

The gun in my hand clicked, the bolt slammed back.

The clip was empty. I pulled the trigger again, enjoying the relative silence. *Click.* I watched my hand on the gun, pulling the trigger. Prints on the gun. *You're pegged, buddy.* Everything clicked. It was a crazy hunch but worth it. I adjusted my ear protection and moved toward the door, peeking through the window and into the storefront of the range. Charlie was alone, no customers. I reloaded.

Movies never tell the truth about how loud handguns are. A .45 automatic is ear-splittingly loud in a small room without ear protection. I left the ears on, held my gun lightly, and stepped through the door. Charlie looked up at me and smiled. I saw her mouth move but I could barely make out the words.

I brought the .45 above my head and squeezed off a shot into the ceiling. Charlie's hands went instinctively to her ears as the entire store rattled in repercussion. The ceiling tile shattered and we were both showered with brilliant bits of gypsum, white powder everywhere, like a concentrated snowstorm. I aimed the gun at her and stepped forward. Her eyes were darting, her body lurching for the reach.

"Don't!" I screamed, and got even closer. Her hand was inches from her belt and the .38 she always wore on her waist. "Don't even fucking move, Charlie."

"What the hell's wrong with you, Dave?" she shouted. "You know I can take you out before you can squeeze off a shot."

"So why didn't you? You had the chance."

She paused a second. "What do you want. The register? I know where you live, man—"

"Speak up, Charlie. Who is it?"

"Who's what?"

I shot the ceiling again. Charlie cringed, hands on her ears.

"Who is it, Charlie?" I was yelling to be heard over her ringing ears. "Who is it?"

"I don't know!" she screamed. "Don't fucking kill me, Dave, just don't fucking kill me!"

I slipped off my ears but held the gun on her. "I'm not gonna kill you, Charlie, I just have to know what you know."

"I don't know shit, man, I'm just trying to get by. They threatened my little girl, my daughter. Can you understand that?"

"Who, Charlie? I need to know *who*."

"I don't fucking know who they are. They jumped me over a year ago."

"What do they want from you?"

"Your guns, man, that's all. Just your guns. They offered me money. I said, *Fuck you, this is my business.* Then they jumped me, said they'd hurt my little girl." She looked at me with genuine fear in her eyes, this tough, frighteningly lethal woman, scared shitless. "She spends the weekends with my ex-husband. I can't protect her all the time. My ex is dirt—you know that. All I got is my daughter and my store. I didn't have a choice, Dave, you gotta believe me."

"Charlie, how does it work?"

"They give me a gun. You know, sometimes you want to try a new gun, you ask me for a suggestion?"

"Yeah."

"They ask me what kind of guns you've been shooting. This guy comes in, he gives me a gun—something you'd like—he leaves. And I keep it here and don't let no one touch it but you. I say, *Try this.* You shoot it, I put it in a bag, when the guy comes back I give it to him. That's all I know."

"Who's the guy?"

"I don't know his name, I swear it."

"What's he look like?"

"Tall, dark hair, a real snake."

Conrad. "How many times, Charlie? How many guns have they given you?"

"Four. Four guns, four pickups."

"You sitting on anything now? That PPK you tried to sell me on?"

"No, Dave, I just thought you'd like it. I swear."

"*When.* When were the guns?"

She leaned on the counter, head shaking. "The first one was last year, very beginning of the year, right after New Year's. Then another last winter, maybe November or December. Then another maybe a month ago, not even. Then last week."

"When last week?"

"When you wanted to shoot the Mini Cougar and I suggested you try the 9mm Baby Glock."

"I made your life easy."

"Well, yeah." She wasn't proud. "But the guy came to get it, David. Just the other day. He was like, *Nice doing business.* I thought that was it, man—I thought it was over. When you came back and asked to shoot it again I gave you a Glock 19, hoping you wouldn't notice."

I hadn't. I lowered the gun. "All right, Charlie. Sorry about your ceiling."

"I'm sorry, Dave. I hope I didn't get you into trouble, but my little girl—"

"I would've done the same thing in your place."

"I'm sorry."

"Forget it. And Charlie, keep a low profile."

"You think I'm in some shit?"

"You're definitely in some shit. I don't know how it will pan out. You could get charged as an accessory in some murders."

"Damnit, Dave, I can't—I have to get out of town—"

"Charlie, calm the fuck down. You can't go anywhere. If the law comes looking for you, you tell them the same story you told me. Because I promise you—if anyone comes for you, you'll be lucky if it's the cops. If you get heat from the other side, you're cooked."

"What are you into?"

"I have no idea. But I keep meeting people who wind up dead. Keep your head down, business as usual. Don't do anything out of the ordinary. I was never here today. This didn't happen."

"All right, Dave. Be careful."

"Watch your back, Charlie." I was already gone.

I went home and tried to forget that there were cameras in my house. If I was still being watched—and I had to assume that I was—the best thing was to go on about my business until I could figure it all out. I would have to play it cool, keep up appearances. And tonight I was definitely in for the evening.

I tried to replicate my usual routine—or what had been my usual routine before all the madness began. I cooked a meal, spent a little time with the paper, had a couple slim fingers of whiskey, and went to bed early. I left the light in the living room on, as usual, got into bed, reading for a few minutes longer, and then turned off my bedside lamp. I hoped the cameras didn't have night vision.

I got up, stuffed my pillows and an extra blanket under my sheets, slipped into my clothes, into the dark hallway, and downstairs to the garage. I let myself out the back door and walked down to Grand to get a cab.

17

There are only three long blocks between Hollywood Billiards and the 711 Club on the south side of Market. I let the cabbie hold a hundred-dollar bill and asked him to wait. It had been years since I'd been back to the 711, a genuine dingy hole of a bar, a narrow shotgun leading into the depths of one's own bile-filled liver. I bellied up to the all-too-familiar dismay and nodded to the old-timer who had served me an infinite number of bracers back in the day.

"Hey there," he grunted. "Long time."

"That it has," I replied. No post-AA judgment from this gentleman. He didn't ask, he didn't tell. The kind of discretion that comes from a lifetime of serving newspapermen. "Frank, I'm expecting a call here."

"I'll keep an ear out."

I nursed a whiskey and waited. At about twenty after ten the phone rang. Frank answered it and put the phone on the bar, nodding at me.

"Yeah?"

"Mr. Crane?" Big Al, no mistaking it.

"Talk to me."

"He's on his way over. We'll be leaving in a couple minutes. Soon as he gets here."

"Good. I'll call you at home tomorrow and tell you how it went." I hung up, knocked it back, tipped Frank, and walked out. I got back into my cab and had the driver pull me up close—but not too close—to Al's jalopy, which hadn't moved since the afternoon. Within a few minutes, Al and Conrad came around the corner and got in.

It was cliché, but there was nothing else to say. "Follow that car."

We got on the 101 and headed south, past South City, finally getting off at Poplar and cruising surface streets into the upscale section of San Mateo that might as well have been Burlingame. All the houses were big, ugly, Northern Californian takes on McMansions. Stucco and pink ruled the day.

Al turned onto a dead-end street. Before following them down, I had the driver stop. I saw Al pull up in front of a big house in the center of the cul-de-sac at the end of the road. Conrad got out and went around the side of the house—there must have been an in-law unit in the back. I had the driver roll down the next block before I paid the fare and sent him away.

I got close to the house and found a nice little hedge and settled in for a long wait. In less than half an hour Conrad came back out, whistling, jumped into Al's car, and took off.

I waited a bit longer, until a few dogs in the neighborhood started barking it up. I didn't want it to be too quiet. I carefully worked my way around the side of the house and saw the in-law unit, a tiny, one-story miniature house. The lights were on inside, and the large French doors in front of the place were well illuminated. I could see a figure moving around inside and ducked out of sight.

The front door opened and the figure emerged: midtwenties, dark complexion, thin but wiry. He was lighting a cigarette and talking on a cell phone.

"*Sí. Una hora y media, más or menos. Voy a tener un pizza, quieres?* Okay, okay. *Entonces no te espero. Ciao.*"

He hung up and dialed another number. He spoke in a slow, hesitant English with a Latino accent.

"Yes, I want one pizza. With pepperoni, and also I want extra cheese. Okay. Can you bring—do you know the Shell station?" He described the location—I'd seen it on the way in. He didn't even want a pizza delivered to this place. That worked for me—if he wasn't meeting anyone for an hour and a half, and if his pizza came in thirty minutes or so, I might have a chance to take a look while he was out grabbing his dinner.

I went back to the hedge and dug in.

About twenty minutes went by and I heard his shuffling footsteps on the sidewalk. He was wearing a crappy pair of sandals, the kind that are common in Mexico and usually made with recycled tire rubber. As soon as he was out of sight I ducked around to the back house.

The door was locked, but not seriously. There was only a simple lockset keeping the French doors closed, and no dead bolt. A quick movement of a credit card and I was in.

The front room was your basic living room, cluttered with empty Pepsi bottles and discarded pizza boxes. This guy liked his pizza. I moved into the back bedroom and almost fell over with shock.

The "deer blind" was a technological behemoth. The simple little back house in a nondescript suburban neighborhood had been tricked out with every imaginable high-tech gadgetry, and the cumulative effect was an enormous electrical shrine with only one object of adulation: me.

A series of monitors displayed my house in South San Francisco in Technicolor: my kitchen, my living room, my bedroom, and my office. With the exceptions of my garage, my bathroom, and the very front vestibule of my house—the tiny foyer that leads off the front door—my entire home was on display. Another monitor showed a map of the Bay Area, with an inset that was a close-up on South San Francisco and a blinking green dot at the center. It was a GPS tracking system, and the blinking dot was right on top of my garage. My car, of course. As near as I could tell, the videos were all being recorded, hard drives ticking and whirring, and one machine was set up to record voices, its monitor displaying a virtual mixing deck and a digital bandwidth. They had my shit wired for sound too.

I still had no earthly idea what these people wanted from me, but they didn't want me dead. Whoever I was dealing with had spent a great deal of time and money keeping track of me, and clearly wanted me left alive. As tempted as I was to stay the hell away from South San Francisco and my televised life, my gut was telling me to get the hell out of there, go home, and keep up appearances. At least now I knew just exactly how low I had to duck to stay below the radar.

I found my way home in a daze.

I couldn't sleep, didn't want to sleep. I haunted my house, walking around my bedroom in the dark, revolving it all. I took the whiskey down to the garage and flipped the light on—no one could see me down there. It had already been the longest, strangest day of my life. Everything had taken a turn for the surreal.

I grabbed a creeper and a shop light and slid under my car. It didn't take long to find it—a small metal box, spot-welded to the chassis, far enough back that I wouldn't have noticed it during a routine oil change. A tracker. Sobczyk was right: they had my car bugged too. I got a grinder and worked quickly through the welds. The box came off and I set it on the floor of the garage, right under where it had been attached to the car.

There was some good news: I'd taken Ashley's painting straight to my garage before opening it, so it was possible that no one knew I had it. They'd been watching my car's movements, but not mine. I'd been making most of my phone calls on the run, and hadn't been driving that much. I had parked several blocks away from Masello's house; I had left my car at Twin Peaks and walked to Katie's shop in West Portal; I had taken public transportation to Chinatown, back to West Portal, and to Rider and Sobczyk's place. There was no reason to believe that any of them were in imminent danger, and no real reason to believe that anyone knew where I'd been or what I'd been up to when I was out of my house and out of my car. Conrad no longer believed I was off the case, but he didn't seem concerned. Sharkskin must have killed the Daltons, but he wasn't after me. For once, I felt like I might have the upper hand. I knew about the deer blind, I had the tracker from my car and could decide whether or not I wanted them to know where I was. I knew about Charlie, I knew I was being set up, and I knew that, somehow, Conrad was connected to everything. And I knew how to get to him.

I opened the garage door and hopped into Delores. I was going for a drive.

18

I met Reuben in the Tenderloin years ago. I had been heading up Leavenworth toward my apartment in Nob Hill, on my way back from working out at the YMCA. He had a shopping cart full of crap stopped in the middle of the street, and was trying to get a crack pipe lit with a wet book of matches. Black, ragged, and ageless—could have been a hard thirty or a blessed sixty. He asked me if I had a light, and I waited for him to give me back my lighter while he smoked. What was surprising, and what got me talking to him, was that he offered me a hit.

He was the highest-functioning crackhead I'd ever met. He was in and out of shelters, but occasionally held down busboy jobs and was incredibly personable. He considered himself a "good" crackhead, and said he "never ripped off anyone who didn't rip me off first." He knew the street, could tell a hard-liner from a tourist and a good cop from a crooked one. He wasn't a rat, but he had a conscience, and when bad things happened he didn't keep his mouth shut. He became a great rock-bottom contact when I was still on the Metro desk.

Reuben once told me that he knew every stripper and prostitute in San Francisco. As he put it, "Ain't one of them don't hit the pipe now and then." Reuben would need a little encouragement, and bribing crackheads with money just gets them to run from you that much quicker. They get money, they want to score.

I parked on Valencia and walked around to 16th and Mission. The block was oddly quiet, and I questioned my luck. As I neared the southwest corner I saw a couple of black guys lurking by the bench. I had to pee, so I went into the public restroom, the curved door sliding open on a disgusting scene, a private space set in a public place that had been used for one too many indiscretions. I did my thing, pulled a ten-dollar bill out of my wallet and palmed it, walked out, and almost ran right into a steeplejack of a man.

"What," he barked at me.

"Just lookin' for a ten-dollar rock."

He grunted and cocked his head at the skinny guy on the bench. He had cornrows, and his chin jutted out slightly, continuously moving back and forth. He was cracked out of his mind, and he was the Man. The steeplejack was his muscle.

"Lookin' for a ten-dollar rock."

What came out of his mouth was completely unintelligible. His lips barely opened.

"What?"

"Are. You. The po-lice."

White guy, well-dressed, trying to score. I get it. "No, man, I ain't a cop."

"Show me your ID."

There was no chance I was pulling out my wallet on this corner. "I'm not showing you my fucking ID."

"Then show me your pipe."

"I don't have a pipe, man, I'm gonna twist that shit up in a joint."

A moment passed. I would say that he thought it over, but there was nothing in those dead eyes that suggested thought. Without telegraphing any intent, without a blink or a warning, he turned his head and spat. A white blur flew out of his mouth and landed on the gray, polished sidewalk. I shrugged and reached my hand out to pass him the money.

He jumped in his seat. "Don't fucking HAND it to me. Drop that shit on the ground."

I dropped the bill on the sidewalk, turned, stooped quickly to pick up the plastic-wrapped rock he'd spit out, and walked away.

I cut around the corner to a bodega that, I figured, would have the necessary paraphernalia. Tiny roses, packaged in small glass tubes, corked on each end, were prominently displayed on the counter next to the register, along with fun-sized candy bars. Crackhead heaven. I bought a rose and asked the half-asleep attendant for some Brillo. He handed me what I needed and charged me a couple of bucks without a sideways glance.

I drove around, then stopped by the Rose Hotel on 6th and Howard, but the desk attendant didn't know Reuben and no one holding down the pavement outside seemed to want to help. I took a slow drive around the corner, down an especially urine-stained block of Minna, but there was no action. I cut across Market and made slow laps through the Tenderloin.

I was coming down Jones, just crossing O'Farrell, when I saw a group of guys in hoodies, leaning against a gated door and sending furtive glances up and down the street. It seemed promising, and when I pulled up one of them approached me. A white guy in an obnoxious car—it wasn't hard to imagine what I was looking for, and he asked.

"Pussy or drugs?"

"Neither. Looking for Reuben."

"Don't know him."

"It's worth five to me if you do."

"Cop?"

"No. Tell him Itchy is looking for him."

"I tole you, don't know the guy."

"You just lost ten bucks."

"You said five."

"See ya."

I pulled out and to the end of the block, stopping at the light. I heard the guy's sneakers on the pavement as he caught up.

"Give me ten, I get you Reuben."

"You get me Reuben, I give you ten."

"I know where he at. Come back in fifteen."

I took a long, slow block. I pulled out the glass tube from the bodega, removed the corks, shook out the tiny fake rose, and tossed it aside. I stuffed the small chunk of Brillo into one end of the tube, shoving it about a third of the way down. An attractive brunette pulled up to me in a convertible with the top up and offered me a smile. I smiled back, gave her a hand signal saying, *Take the top down,* and she shook her head and laughed as I turned left at the red light. When I was stopped again I unwrapped the crack rock and set it in the console next to the newly minted pipe.

Fifteen minutes later, Reuben was riding shotgun. I handed him the rock and the pipe and took a slow ride up Taylor.

"Man, Itchy Crane! Where the hell you been!" Reuben had lost another tooth by the looks of it, but he was as jovial as ever. "Can't believe you remembered my favorite flavor!" He snapped the rock in half, dropped it into the pipe, and took a deep hit.

"Reuben, keep your head down. We're in a convertible."

"No sweat, I know all the cops 'round here." He reloaded. "But why you give that asshole ten? Anyone else woulda found me for two." The economics offended him. That, and the fact that someone else had ten of my dollars that could have been his.

"I didn't have time to fuck around," I said. "Don't worry, I got fifty for you if you can find out what I need."

"Fifty?" He grinned, a wide grin with gaping holes. "Anything for my man Itchy."

"There's a girl who dances at Market Street. Name of Karyn, Karyn with a y. I need to find her."

"You know where she works. Drop by."

"I can't go to her work, all right? But I want her. I want to know where she lives, or where she hangs out after hours."

"Karyn with a y . . . what does she look like?"

"Redhead. Big tits."

"Yeah . . ." He took a hit and held it in, talking without breathing. "Real sweet-looking?"

I nodded.

"I think I know her."

"Tell her I'll pay her five hundred bucks for a couple hours of her time."

He spat out smoke and started coughing. "Five hunnerd? You crazy? You can get pussy for—"

"I didn't say I wanted to sleep with her." Economics. Reuben hated to see people overcharged. "I said, tell her she'll get five hundred. No sex. Just a couple hours. I need her to take a ride with me."

"You got it."

"And Reuben, don't use my name, all right? Tell her my name is Dan."

"Dan. You got it."

"You sure? You can find her?"

"No bullshit, Itchy, I know this girl. I tole you," he said, singing it, *"I know every ho in San Francis-co."* He let out a rattling, backfiring spasm of amusement. "I'll get her this morning, see about the wheres and whens, and you call me at my sister's place."

"Your sister got her own place now?"

He nodded, too busy with the pipe to speak.

"That's great." I took down the number. "You want me to drive you back down?" We were almost at Columbus.

"Naw," he said. "Since we here, I wanna go to the Lusty Lady! They got this new girl, she got so many tattoos! It don't make my dick hard, but . . ." He shrugged. "Something about her, you know?"

"Women are mysterious creatures."

"You know that's right. And it only cost a quarter to look."

I let him out and went home, pulled quietly into my garage, slipped the tracker into the glove box, and snuck up the stairs in the dark and into my bed.

19

I woke up around noon, feeling more hungover than if I'd actually been hungover. I made some coffee, casually pacing the kitchen as I waited for it to brew, not quite awake and only gently, almost blithely aware that I was being watched. How banal, how boring. How many such empty, everyday moments had been recorded—just me, alone in my house; my quiet, uncompelling life. I stirred sugar into my coffee and was irritated by a bit of crust in the corner of my eye. High drama in the Crane household. I went into the bathroom and threw some water on my face, and it suddenly hit me like a ton of bricks.

My alibi.

I ran down to the Schoolhouse Deli and called the *Chronicle*.

"Give me Thomas Grange." Horrible hold muzak, an anxious pause.

"Tom Grange."

"Tom, you on deadline? It's David Crane."

"Itchy, wow, this is a blast from the past. I got a minute. How are you?"

"I've been better. Listen, I need a favor."

"Big or small?"

"Just some info."

"Shoot."

"I need you to check the archives for any unsolved homicides close to these dates . . . you ready?"

"Go."

"January 1, 1996, November 15, 1996, and August 18, 1997." The dates from the three paintings.

"Anything in particular I should be looking for?"

"Nope. Yes or no: were there any homicides in the Bay Area on these dates."

"Easy. Give me ten."

Tom was a good guy, honest, and not a drunk. One of the few people I knew from the paper who wasn't a complete scumbag. Gay, basically married, two dogs. I paced and smoked a couple and called him back.

"Yeah, David, you're right on the money. Let's see, New Year's Day, '96 . . . looks like just before two a.m. *Alberto Martiartu, fifty-two, became the first murder victim of 1996. He was shot in the head in the hallway of the Dudley Apartments at 172 6th Street* . . . Says he was a Cuban immigrant with twenty-one aliases. Still unsolved. And just this past August . . . *Lucius Rodgers, twenty-four, was shot at 8:55 a.m. in the driveway of his home* . . . *as he sat in his parked pickup in East Oakland listening to music, police said.* No suspects, no motive. And this other one you have to remember: November 15, 1996. *A BMW hit a hydrant at Steiner and Post streets. The driver was dead with a bullet in his back.*"

I felt a cold shiver. "Really."

"Yeah. Defense attorney Dennis Natali. Remember? They found all these connections between him and— what was the guy's name? Here it is, *Vietnamese gang boss Cuong Tran.*"

I did remember. Natali was good friends with the DA, Terence Hallinan, and divided his time between attending high-class political fundraisers and defending alleged gangsters. Tran was big-time in the Tenderloin.

"That was a strange situation," Tom said. "They were killed within minutes of each other. Says here cops found a phone number on Natali's pager that led them to suspects in the Tran killing. And Natali had represented one of Tran's codefendants in an earlier beef. But they haven't solved it. This one is still out there."

"Thanks, Tom, that helps a lot."

"What's this for?"

"Some college kid's research paper. Thanks again. I'll be in touch."

It wasn't just about the Daltons—there were other murders. The dates on the paintings matched up with three unsolved murders, and they matched when Charlie had handed off the guns to Conrad. They use a gun for a murder, they give it to Charlie, they get my prints, I'm a patsy.

Ashley did love me. The paintings—the surveillance—were my alibi. The scenes depicted in the paintings may not have been at the precise moments of the murders, but the flash drives told the whole story. I was home at the exact time of each murder. I would never have been able to explain my whereabouts. They were watching me to know when I was in a position to be suckered. But the surveillance itself proved I couldn't have done it. The painting I didn't have—the one Conrad took from the Dalton Gallery—must have another flash drive proving my innocence of the New Year's Day killing.

But Conrad said I was also being set up for the Dalton murders and I couldn't figure out how. Maybe the 9mm Baby Glock had something to do with it. No, I'd used it on the range—just hours *before* Dalton got hit. For Susan, I was already cleared. Maybe Conrad was bluffing, or they used one of the first three guns to kill the Daltons, or Charlie was lying, or all of the above, or none.

It didn't matter. I was in deep shit. Why would anyone want to frame me for a murder—or several, for that matter? And why was I hired to find the girl who was trying to save me? I wondered which side McCaffrey was playing on and whether there were more than two sides.

And my guardian angel had vanished. I still didn't know who Ashley was, how she fit into anything, or where to find her. But now I knew she was looking out for me. Whoever she was, she was trying to help. I wanted to meet her more than ever.

I went home and picked up the phone to call McCaffrey. His secretary put me on hold for a good five minutes, but I didn't let it bother me.

"Itchy, what can I do you for?"

"McCaffrey, I don't think I'm going to be able to find your girl for you."

"What? What's this about?"

"Look, you gave me nothing, I got lucky with a lead at a gallery—"

"You did. What happened?"

"Nothing. It was a wash."

I let that drift across the line like tumbleweed on an Old West picture set. Something about the silence told me he knew otherwise.

"A wash?"

"Yeah. Turned out to be nothing. Listen, I just don't think this girl wants to be found. I haven't talked to anyone who's seen her. She's either dead or long gone. She's not in San Francisco, McCaffrey, and the trail is ice cold." He didn't say anything. "You want me to deduct my expenses, give you your money back?"

"No, no, keep the cash, Itchy. That was the deal."

"Well . . . sorry I couldn't be of more help."

"That's all right. Thanks for trying."

Of course it was bullshit. There was no way in hell I was off the case, not now, but I wanted whoever was listening to believe that I'd had enough, and that, if nothing else, I was no longer looking for Ashley. Maybe it would give me some breathing room. There was no way out of this case but through it; I couldn't walk away.

I took a long, hot shower, put on some comfortable clothes, and double-checked that the tracker was in Delores's glove box. Let them watch. I drove down Spruce to the strip mall at El Camino and parked in front of the Albertson's. I walked across the lot to an electronics store and bought a pay-as-you-go cell phone, the kind that doesn't require a credit card to secure. I needed a phone number, and no one would be able to trace this line to me.

I called Al at home.

"Mr. Crane, did it go all right last night?"

"It went great, Al. I owe you some money. Will you be at Hollywood tonight?"

"Sure."

"I'll stop by."

I called Reuben at his sister's place.

"Itchy," he said, cackling, "I got yer ho. It's her day

off today too, so she's waitin' to hear from you."

"Fantastic. I owe you money, Reuben."

"Ain't no thing. You call my sister next time you're in the City, drop it by here. I owe her plenty of back rent."

He gave me Karyn's cell phone number and I called her up.

"Karyn?"

"Is this Dan?"

"This is."

"Reuben said you were looking for a date."

"I am. What are you doing this afternoon?"

"Waiting for you." She was good at playing coy.

"It'll be late. I live in the East Bay. Where will you be?"

"I don't know, sugar, why don't you call me when you're on your way?"

"I will."

I walked back over to the Albertson's, did some leisurely grocery shopping, went home, and cooked a big breakfast of bacon, sausage, hash browns, fried eggs, and sourdough toast. I settled into my kitchen and read the paper back to front, ate slowly, made coffee, smoked cigarettes, and luxuriated in relaxation. Then I took a nap.

20

It was almost dusk and a little cool, the sky bright blue with high scattered clouds. I rode Delores along 101, top down as usual, feeling the wind in my face. I was almost at ease. I'd made a few trips to the basement, coming back up with grease on my hands, worrying a rag and holding random car parts. I even went so far as to put in a call to Gotelli's to get a quote on a new carburetor. Hopefully, whoever was on duty at the deer blind would believe I was working on my car. I left the tracker on my workbench.

Karyn was expecting me. I figured with the proper persuasion—namely, the right amount of money—I could find out whatever she knew about Conrad, and, more importantly, convince her to get more information out of him. Conrad had a habit with this girl, and that made her his weakness.

I made a quick stop in the Tenderloin and paid off Reuben's sister on my way to North Beach. I'd told Karyn to meet me at Tosca. I've always liked the place: its red vinyl booths, the enormous cappuccino machines, the signature coffee cocktails lined up on the bar waiting to be served, the opera and jazz on the jukebox. Besides, it's in the heart of strip-club central, Karyn would know it, and no one would notice me and a stripper having a chat.

Karyn was easy to spot, perched on a barstool, putting on the face of an innocent, wearing too much lipstick and a full-length white faux-fur coat. She looked ridiculous, but no worse than half the hipsters in the room. It was still early, and the bar was only half full, still bringing in a mild happy-hour crowd. I went right up to the bar and sat on the stool next to hers.

"Karyn?" Half of her lip turned up at the edge. "I'm Dan. Reuben's friend?"

She gave a full-fledged smile. "Hi. You're much better looking than Reuben said you'd be."

"Reuben never found me attractive. Let's get a booth."

"Um . . ." She tapped the bar top and looked at me expectantly. I realized she hadn't yet ordered a drink.

"Where are my manners?" I got us a round and maneuvered her into a booth.

It didn't take her long to get around to the eternal preoccupation: "Reuben said you wanted to give me five hundred dollars."

I pulled out a cigarette but didn't light it. "That's true. I want . . . some of your time." I was reaching for my lighter when my phone started going off. I hadn't given anyone the number. "Excuse me," I said, "would you give me just a second?"

"Take your time."

I booked it outside. "Hello?"

"Mr. Crane? It's Al."

"Al? How the hell did you get this number?"

"I have caller ID, you called me from this number—I just took a chance."

Of course. "What is it, Al?"

"It's Conrad. He's on his way over here."

"To your place?"

"Yeah. He's hopping mad. I don't know what happened, but he said we're paying you a visit. Something's wrong. I never heard him like this."

"You're coming over now?"

"Soon as he gets here we're going to your house."

"All right." My mind was flipping possibilities like a card counter in Reno. "Al—why did you call me?"

"I don't want to see anything bad happen."

"Try to stall him a bit, will you?"

"I'll do what I can."

Karyn was chewing on her cocktail straw when I sidled back into the booth. "Sorry about that," I said. "Business never stops."

"I don't mind." She gave me a coquettish smile. "So, you were saying?"

I had to improvise, and quick. I slipped out a hundred-dollar bill. "Come with me to my place. Here's a hundred, just for taking a ride with me. There's four more in it for you if you like what I like, and if you don't, no offense, I'll bring you home."

"No sex?"

"Absolutely no sex. Mostly I just want to talk."

She shifted in her seat and pulled her coat close to her. "Well . . . I usually don't do this, but Reuben said you were a nice guy."

Karyn, like many women, loved the idea of riding in a convertible. She leaned her head back and screamed the minute we got onto the highway. As the mood flattened out, she pulled out a pack of 100s and looked at me for a light. I took her cigarette and leaned toward the windshield to get it lit. I handed it to her, put the heater on, and rolled up my window. She smoked and smiled.

"Karyn, how did you get into this business?"

"Same as everyone, I guess," she replied without emotion. "I was in school and I needed money, and I thought, how about stripping?"

"I thought it was a little more than just stripping at Market Street."

"Some of the girls will do anything in the back room, but it's really up to the girl. I usually don't do that stuff, if that's what you're wondering."

"No—I don't mean to make you uncomfortable, I'm just curious."

"Well, there is one guy I give full service on a regular basis." She giggled. "But I kind of like him. And I didn't give him full service the first time he came in, only after he kept asking for me."

"Who's the lucky guy?" Like I didn't know the answer.

"Conrad." She was gushing. "He says he's crazy about me, but a lot of guys say that. You know, it's not so bad, really. You give enough hand jobs and it's just like another massage. But clients say crazy shit just to try to get more out of you."

"I bet."

"They're the same as we are, really," she said, flicking her cigarette out of the car. "You should hear what some of the girls say to guys, just to get them to give them more money."

I could imagine, but I was too busy thinking about what I was going to say to Conrad to keep him from killing us both.

21

We came in through the garage and went upstairs. Karyn asked for the bathroom and I grabbed my .45 and stuffed it down the back of my pants. I called out, "I can't believe you just happened to be in the neighborhood!"

"What?" Karyn yelled through the door, and I ignored her. It was ridiculous that I was trying to keep up appearances—my cover was going to be blown in the next few minutes. I made sure the front door wasn't locked and made myself comfortable on the couch. When Karyn came out I asked her to do a little private dance for me. She moved close, played at kissing me, rubbed my knee, pulled away, and lost a piece of clothing. She seemed to be in her comfort zone and I tried to drag the moment out. She was down to her bra and panties before curiosity got to her.

"So what did you want that was so special? You could see this at the Cinema."

"Just give me another minute," I said. "I like this."

She moved her hips and bit her index finger.

They weren't trying to be sneaky. I heard Alan's beat-up jalopy pull up outside, and I heard both car doors slam.

"Come here," I said to Karyn. "Come sit on my lap." I pulled the .45 out of my pants as she tittered and parked her moneymaker. I held her close, but not too close. I heard footsteps climbing up my stairs. I imagined Conrad barging in, killing me in my own house. I nuzzled my nose into Karyn's neck and waited. The screen door creaked.

I spoke: "Come on in, Conrad, I've been expecting you." I held the gun next to Karyn's exposed midriff. Conrad sauntered in, unarmed.

"How ya doin', Itchy?" Then he saw his girl on my lap and stopped cold.

"Conrad?" Karyn was confused. "What are you doing here?"

"You see what I see?" I said, moving my eyes to my .45. He held his hands out.

"Itchy, now—"

"What? What is it?" Karyn looked down and saw the gun. I heard her lungs expand.

"Don't scream, Karyn," I cautioned. "I don't want to hurt you but I can't say what might happen if I get startled."

"Karyn, baby, don't move," Conrad said in the calmest, most concerned voice I'd heard from him. "Itchy is an old friend of mine, we're just going to have a little chat. Be calm."

"I'm scared, Connie."

"Don't be scared, just . . . just keep your mouth shut." She settled down, and Conrad showed me his palms.

"Well," I said, "we're all nice and comfortable."

"I just thought I'd drop by." Conrad had found his balls, the slither coming back into his voice.

"If I'd known you were coming I'd have made a pot of coffee."

"Looks to me like you knew I was coming. Did he know, Al?"

Al appeared next to Conrad, brandishing his Colt. "I dunno," he muttered.

"Alan, nice of you to join us."

"Drop it, Itchy," Conrad rasped. "Drop the fucking gun already."

"No thanks, it makes me feel more comfortable. I don't like Al standing in an open doorway with a gun, though. Neighbors could be bad for all of us. Shut the door behind you, Al."

Al didn't move. Conrad cocked his head at him, and Al shut the door. They were both still standing in the vestibule.

"You fellas want to come in and have a seat?"

"We're fine right here," Conrad sneered.

"Let me guess," I said, "you don't want the guys watching the surveillance cameras to know that you're here."

"I don't know what you're talking about."

"Really? That's funny—see, Karyn, honey, I should give you a little background. Conrad here works for some guys who have my house wired with cameras. That little dance you were doing for me earlier? It's all on tape."

She furrowed her brow. "I don't like that."

"I don't like it either, darling. But Conrad seems to have forgotten that the place is wired for sound too. They might not be able to see you, Connie, but they can hear us."

"No," he spat. "There's no sound in this room. Just your office."

I hadn't had that long to investigate and couldn't be sure. "You're bluffing."

"Believe what you want. Al, you think you can shoot him without hitting Karyn?"

I didn't let Al answer. "Forget it, Connie. I flinch, Karyn bleeds. Can't we just talk?" He didn't answer but he didn't argue. "Help me out with this one, Connie. You and Al come over here to scare me off. You don't kill me. I track you down, and you tell me that I killed Susan Dalton, when we both know I didn't. And now you're back and Al's still holding a gun on me. What gives?"

"Itchy." Conrad was getting testy, but leaned against the wall casually, glancing out the window. "Put the fucking gun on the table. We both know you're not gonna kill her."

"You're probably right." I nudged the nose of the gun against Karyn's hip, toying with the strap of her panties.

"Stop it," she giggled, "that's cold!"

"But I might just put one in her leg and see how much that turns you on."

"You're the one who's bluffing."

"The Dalton lady and I had a bit of a thing going," I said. "Someone killed her. Maybe you. It would only be fair balance if something happened to *your* girl."

He thought it over. He didn't like it much. "I didn't kill Ms. Dalton."

"Didn't think so."

"What did she tell you about Ashley?"

"Mmm, that name isn't ringing any bells."

"Shoot him, Al."

"Al, don't be stupid. Conrad, Susan Dalton didn't know a damn thing about Ashley. She knew less than her brother, and he knew nothing."

"Who hired you to find Ashley?"

"She's dead, don't you know?"

"Don't give me that bullshit. Who hired you to find Ashley?"

"You must be kidding. You don't even know who hired me? Is that why you came here tonight?"

Conrad's eyes narrowed to slits. "Charlie left town, asshole." I wanted to groan; I had bet on Charlie to play it cool. "So you must have got to her. How much you know decides whether or not I let you live."

"I can't see how you're in a position to make demands. I wouldn't have known about Charlie if you hadn't told me they had my fingerprints on guns."

Conrad worked his jaw. "I might have . . . overstepped my bounds a little."

"Who's setting me up?"

"I can't help you, Itchy."

"Who's setting me up? Who wired my house, who's framing me for murder?"

"Who hired you to find Ashley?"

"I can't help you, Connie."

"Shoot him, Al."

Al didn't move.

"Shoot him."

"I don't want to hurt anyone, Conrad." Al's voice seemed to be coming from far away.

"Just fucking—who's paying you here?" Conrad demanded.

"Guess you don't pay him enough," I offered.

"Al, what's your goddamn problem? Itchy, what'd you do to my muscle? Al, just kill him."

Al lowered his gun a little and looked at Conrad,

eyes soft, like a little boy. "I told you, Conrad, I'm not killin' nobody."

Karyn shifted her weight on my lap. "I have to pee," she whispered.

"Just a little while longer," I said. "We're almost done."

"Al," Conrad snarled, "give me your gun and go wait in the car."

Al passed him the Colt. "Sorry, Mr. Crane," he said.

"Don't worry about a thing."

Al opened the door, squeezing his large body past Conrad in the tiny foyer, and went out.

Conrad raised the Colt. "Itchy motherfucking Crane, tell me who fucking hired you before I put you out of your misery."

"Fuck you," I said. "You won't risk hurting the girl. Now tell me who's setting me up, and why."

"Can't do it." He shook his head vehemently. "I love you, Karyn, but you don't understand what they'll do to me if Itchy fucks this up."

"You . . . love me?" Karyn was melting, misunderstanding the severity of the moment.

"You know the people you're working for will kill you for nothing. And if you kill me, they'll know," I said. His eyes were on Karyn and I hoped he was softening. "Tell me who's setting me up, take the girl, and disappear. I got no beef with you, Conrad."

"Can't do it. Tell me who hired you."

"Who are you working for?"

"Who hired you? Was it McCaffrey?"

"We gonna keep this up all night?"

"Do you even know about McCaffrey and the girl?"

"Who's McCaffrey?"

"Itchy, you're dead no matter what, you stupid fuck, don't you fucking get that?"

"And I'm betting so are you."

It was an impasse. We bored eyes into each other, a true cowboy showdown. The girl didn't breathe. Conrad forced air out of his nostrils with a clenched mouth. He lowered the Colt a half-inch and shook his head. "I—" he said, and there was a pop and a faint squish and he flinched. The Colt slowly dropped to his side, and he gave me a lackluster grin. "Fucking. You fucking—" He raised the Colt back up with a monumental effort, and then I heard that faint squish again and I saw a flash of blood speckle the wall behind him. Conrad fell, Colt first, and began bleeding all over my hardwoods.

Karyn's scream split the entire neighborhood in half. She ran to him and I had to bodily pick her up and carry her out of the room, thrashing.

"You want to get shot?" I asked her, and I threw her into the bathroom and locked the door. I ran back into the front room, ducked down below the windows and checked Conrad's carotid. He was fading fast, but he still had a pulse.

I needed to see. I ran outside, keeping low, and saw a car speeding up the street. I started to run after it but only made it a few steps before I tripped over Al, lying in a heap on the side of the road. He was holding his head, which was bleeding, though he didn't appear to have been shot.

"Al, what the fuck?"

He looked up at me with glassy eyes and said, "He hit me." Then he passed out.

I whipped out my cell phone and called information and asked to be directed to an ambulance—I didn't want 911 sending the cops over right away.

I went back inside. Conrad was gone; the second shot had hit him in the neck and he'd bled out. I shut the front door and took Al's Colt out of Conrad's dead hand. I wiped it down good—Al didn't need this heat—and put it back in Conrad's hand, pressing his fingertips all over it. I searched his body and found his wallet—*Conrad Johanssen*, with an address in Noe Valley. There was nothing else of interest—just an ATM and a Blockbuster card.

I waited for the cavalry.

22

"Well, isn't it nice to see Mr. Crane again, Berrera?" Willits asked when they came in. Berrera grunted.

"Wish I could say the same," I remarked. "Investigating a South City incident? A little out of your jurisdiction—surprised you seem so chipper."

"Yeah," Berrera growled, "I love being woken up and dragged down to the station to see an unlicensed dick who's been holding out on us."

"We asked South San Francisco's finest to keep an eye on you," Willits added. "Give us a call if you came up on their radar."

I had a couple things working in my favor. The ambulance had come before any of my neighbors noticed the Samoan bleeding in front of my house. They decreed him stable and sped him off. By then my neighbors were sticking their heads through their curtains—likely calling 911—and I knew I'd never get Karyn into a cab unnoticed. I got her dressed and slipped her a couple of Valiums to calm her down, and managed to talk some sense into her before the cops showed up. She was upset about Conrad, but sufficiently concerned about her own hide to realize that it was better to pretend she didn't know him. In fact, she suggested it. She was worried about a prostitution charge and didn't need anything heavier. We got our stories straight and she left me feeling confident that she'd keep her mouth shut and play along. She was tougher than I'd given her credit for.

The South City cops taped up my house with yellow crime scene banners and drew a chalk outline on my hardwood floor. It was a circus. Karyn and I were both taken into custody, then quickly transferred to downtown SF for grilling. The nice thing about sitting in an interrogation room for two hours waiting for your favorite cops to get out of bed is that you have plenty of time to figure out how much to give them.

"Willits, you're gay, aren't you?" For some reason I felt like getting on his bad side.

"What's that got to do with anything?"

"I was just wondering. I mean, are you the kind of guy who became a cop so that you can stay in the closet for the rest of your life, or are you the sort who likes to wear your uniform to the Castro Street Fair and, you know, work it."

"That's enough," Berrera said, cutting Willits off before he had a chance to respond. "You fuck a chick, she winds up dead, you tell us you know nothing. Now some guy just happens to get shot right in your goddamn doorway, and you're hiding out with a known prostitute. What the hell's going on?"

"Wow, Berrera, that's the most words I've ever heard you speak in a row."

"Itchy," Willits said, "what are you working?"

"Willits, if you think you're gonna score some brownie points by using my nickname as a term of endearment, you're dead fucking wrong. That name was pegged to me as an insult. I don't particularly like it."

"Crane." Berrera was getting impatient. "What the hell are you working?"

"I'm not a private investigator, I'll remind you. I'm an information broker."

"So what kind of information do you have on all these deaths that keep happening around you?" Willits just couldn't keep his mouth shut.

"I told you, I don't have the foggiest. It's a simple missing person case—"

"I thought you weren't a PI," Willits interjected.

"Sorry, a missing person inquiry, and the family won't release the last name, so I honestly don't have any more to tell you than the last time I was in here. I thought I had a lead with Dalton, I was wrong, he got dead, I don't know why. I liked his sister, she got dead, I'm not happy about that but I still don't know why."

"So what about Conrad Johanssen?"

"The dead guy? He stormed into my house, told me he didn't like my business, and offered to take me for a ride."

"A ride where?" Willits asked.

"You know, I kind of forgot to ask. His invitation was of the firearm variety, and I'm more accustomed to pretty paper with fancy calligraphy."

"The Colt found at the scene."

"Yes."

"But the Colt isn't registered to Johanssen," Willits said, "it's registered to an Alan Punihaole." *Al, you dope, you registered your gun?* "You know him?"

"Nope."

"Because we can't seem to find him, and we were hoping you could help."

"Well, if he registered his gun he's probably in the book."

"We had a radio car stop by. He's not home. Owes back rent too."

"Tough break."

"Crane, he's got quite a rap sheet."

"So?"

"So he might be involved."

"Ah," Berrera made a noise like air escaping a corpse, "it's mostly petty shit. Johanssen could have taken the gun off him."

I was ready to leave. "It sounds like you guys have all kinds of theories you need to look into. Are we done?"

Berrera gave Willits a look. Willits turned to me.

"No, Crane, we're not done. We're not happy about being rousted out of bed and brought down here, and we're never happy about a murder—in or out of our jurisdiction. We want to know what you're working, exactly what you're into, and everything you know about the Daltons, about Johanssen, all of it. Or we can charge you with solicitation."

I laughed out loud. "You mean the nice girl that I was on a blind date with tonight? The one I was canoodling on the couch when this asshole barged in and ruined my evening before ruining my hardwoods? We're talking about the same girl, right? The one in the next room telling you nothing?"

They eyed me but didn't say anything.

"I told you, Johanssen threatened me, and somebody shot him. I don't know any more than that. You go do your homework and you'll find that he was shot from the street—surely one of you has heard the word *trajec-*

tory before. You'll also find out that he was shot with—I don't know, something other than a .38 Derringer or a .45 automatic. Those are the only guns I own, and they're both registered. So I didn't shoot him. And you obviously don't like me for the Dalton deaths, so I don't know why you keep bringing them up. I'm a witness, nothing more, so let me know when someone gets arrested or indicted and I'll be happy to do my civic duty. You kids can't hold me and you know it. If I find something that I think you'll like—like what ballerina school this lost little girl went to when she was six—I'll give you a call. And if you find out who killed that sweet Susan Dalton, tell me, coz I'd like to kick him in the balls. Otherwise, how does it go? *If you want to see me, pinch me or subpoena me or something and I'll see you at the inquest—maybe.* Now, if you'll excuse me, *The Maltese Falcon* is on again tonight and I'd like to go home and microwave some popcorn."

I got up and made for the door.

"You know," Berrera said, "you can't hold out on us forever, Itchy."

I left and nobody stopped me.

When I hit the street, Karyn was on the curb smoking a cigarette and pacing. She saw me coming, barked, "You son of a bitch!" and slapped me in the face. I probably deserved it.

"Karyn, I'm sorry for the hassle."

"You got Conrad killed! He was gonna marry me!"

"Conrad got *himself* killed. I only wanted you for leverage—"

She hit me again. "Asshole!" I probably deserved that

too, but I wasn't certain I deserved much more.

"I'm sorry for all of this. What else can I say?"

"You owe me four hundred dollars."

I paid her. "Get out of town, Karyn."

She stormed off, her step more mercenary than grieving.

Cops will take you downtown, but they never offer you a ride home. It was almost midnight, so I called a cab, trying not to think on the way. I stepped over the yellow tape and the bloodstains, poured myself a whiskey, shot it, turned off all the lights, and crawled into bed. Maybe they didn't see Conrad get shot. Maybe they didn't see Conrad at all. But they saw a hysterical stripper and probably heard her scream. Anyone at the deer blind knew that something hinky had gone down in my house tonight.

I got out of bed, fluffed the blankets, and slipped downstairs. I had to see Al.

23

Al had been taken to Kaiser on El Camino, and when I arrived he was under observation. He looked to be in good spirits, propped up against a mass of pillows, idly flipping the channels on the TV suspended on the far side of the room.

"They giving you any good drugs?"

Al gave me a courageous grin. "Not bad. How're you?"

"Staying out of the pokey so far. Can't complain."

"Hey, I really appreciate what you did for me back there. I don't need any more trouble with the cops."

"Thanks for warning me about Conrad. What the hell happened?"

"Dunno. Somebody must've followed us there, or something, coz I didn't see anyone pull up after I got back in my car. Then I see this guy standing in front of your house, and he raises a gun—"

"What kind of gun?"

"Dunno. A pistol, something. So I ducked down, heard the pops, then I peeked and saw him running down the street and into a car. I jumped out to try to read the plate but he put his headlights right on me and hit the gas. Clipped me on the way by."

"You all right?"

"Ah, it's nothin'," he said, waving me off. "Bounced

my head off the pavement. Mild concussion, couple of stitches. No big deal." He was tough, you had to give it to him. "Mr. Crane?"

"Call me David."

"David . . . is he dead?"

"Conrad? Yeah. He was dead in seconds."

Al's face pinched up and I almost thought he would cry. "Too bad. He wasn't a bad guy, y'know? A little crazy, but . . . I made some good money with him." Al's clicking stopped on a Mexican telenovela and we both looked on for a moment.

"So, Al, I gotta ask."

"Yeah?"

"What'd the guy look like?"

"Dunno. Too dark. Wearin' a suit, medium height. Maybe dark."

Sharkskin. No news there. "Anything else you can tell me about tonight?"

"Not much. Conrad found me at the pool hall, said he needed me. I didn't want to do any more work for him. I'm used to just standing there looking tough while somebody else says, *Give me the money you owe me.*" He sighed, almost aware of how stupid it all sounded. "Conrad's meaner than me. And I been asking around the last couple days. Nobody knows nothin' about him. In the Tenderloin, at Hollywood . . . nobody knows nothin'. Some think he's this high roller, some say he's just a poser. Nobody knows who he works for, and nobody knows how he gets his money—but he's always hiring people."

I mulled it over. "Including you."

"Right. I tried to say no, but he wouldn't let me off

the hook, and he paid me up front—it was a lot of money, David."

"Fair enough."

He shrugged. "I thought I could warn you in time, and—well, you said you wanted to find him." Al flicked the channels again, settled on a cartoon. "But he showed up two seconds after I talked to you. He came up to my place to use the phone, and then we left. I couldn't stall 'im."

"You did great, Al. Who did he call?"

Al shook his head. "Dunno. But he asked whoever it was where you were. It was weird. They knew you were home."

Or they thought I was. "Anything else?"

"He said he wasn't going to do anything. He was real sketchy—he was only on the phone for a second, and when he got off he seemed kind of . . ."

"Scared?"

"Rattled, more like. I don't think that guy gets scared."

"*Got* scared."

He looked away. "Yeah."

"What else, Al?"

"Just a lot of muttering. Something about a killing, someone you're supposed to kill." He turned the TV off and looked at me. "You kill people?"

"Al, I've never killed anyone."

"Well . . . whatever happens with all of this, I want in."

"What?"

"I wanna work for you, Mr. Crane. I'd rather be on your side than Conrad's, and—"

"Conrad's dead, my friend."

"And whoever killed him tried to kill me. I feel like I been set up."

"Just rest up."

"But will you keep me in on it?"

I turned this over in my mind for a moment. "Maybe."

"I don't care about the dough, man, I just wanna get these guys."

"Call me if you think of anything else. And Al, do *not* go home. We have to assume they know where you live. Our mystery man knows he hit you, maybe he thinks you're dead. If he finds out otherwise . . . besides, the cops are going to want to ask you about your gun."

"I can stay at my aunt's in Vallejo."

"Call my cell phone when you get somewhere so I know where to find you."

"They said they'd release me in the morning. I'll call you."

"And Al, give me your keys. I might drop by your place."

"They're on the nightstand."

I got up to go and Al flicked the TV back on. "Oh, hey, there was something else," he said. "On the drive over, Conrad kept saying, *That bitch Ashley, that fucking bitch.* Like that. Who's Ashley?"

"I wish I knew."

Back on the stoop of Al's building I was glancing over my shoulder with chilling apprehension. I half-expected the place to be trashed already, and considering the time of night I didn't want to draw any attention. The front door looked intact, so I let myself in quietly and went upstairs, listening for a few minutes at the door to Al's apartment. I opened it up and was relieved to find it looking the same as it had the last time I'd been there. They either thought he was dead or hadn't tracked him down yet. I'd only be a minute.

I found Al's telephone and checked the caller ID. I wanted the number Conrad called, thinking it must have been the deer blind. I expected it to be a 650, for San Mateo, but the last call dialed was to an area code I didn't recognize. I took down the number and got the hell out of there.

I never really imagined Conrad living in Noe Valley. When I found his place, on Clipper between Sanchez and Noe, I couldn't believe my eyes. I expected a lowlife to live like a lowlife. The house was a gorgeous, sand-colored Edwardian with big front windows, peach accents, and subtly detailed moldings; a simple staircase led to the main house, above the garage. I'd kill for a house like that.

I walked back and forth on the sidewalk a few times, poking around, looking for a possible way to break in—when I realized I didn't have to. The front door was slightly ajar. Moving closer, I could see it had been forced open and didn't close correctly. I pushed in and made my way carefully up to the second floor, finding the stairwell door open. I wished I had a gun.

I pushed the door open as slowly and as silently as I could. Whoever had beaten me there was long gone. The place was trashed. Every cabinet was emptied onto the floor, every piece of furniture overturned and ripped open. I picked my way gingerly through the debris, shaking my head. I wasn't going to find anything here.

As concerned as I was about being discovered in such an obvious crime scene, it had been a long day—and a long night—and I really needed a drink. I poked around the detritus of the kitchen and uncovered an unbroken fifth of Ancient Age. *Not bad, Conrad,* I thought. *In another life you and I could have gotten along famously.* I found a plastic cup and poured myself a couple of fingers.

And then, standing in dead Conrad's demolished kitchen, drinking his whiskey out of a Mardi Gras cup from 1992, I spotted it. Hidden in plain view, right out in the open, completely overlooked. Wedged between the refrigerator and the wall was a cylindrical mailing tube, the kind that one uses to send posters, photographs—or paintings.

It was addressed, in lazy, sloppy handwriting, to *El Viejo*—the Old Man—*Hotel del Norte, Puerto Barrios, Guatemala*. It was sealed and ready to go—it just needed postage.

I opened it up and pulled out a rolled-up canvas. It was the post office painting—the one Conrad had taken from the Dalton Gallery in the face of Susan's protests. I spread it out on the kitchen counter and took a close look; the flash drive was still embedded. Why was Conrad sitting on this? Why hadn't he mailed it off?

And a better question: Guatemala? All of Sobczyk's conspiracy talk came flooding back to me in a wave of nausea.

I picked up Conrad's phone, called Pac Bell, and asked a bored-sounding operator about the strange area code that Conrad had dialed from Al's place. "I'm not sure, sir, it could be a cell phone–only code that isn't in our system."

"Cell phone only?"

She exhaled heavily, and responded the way one answers a petulant child: "In some markets, there are so many cell phones that cities are creating new area codes. It could be LA, or New York—like I said, sir, it might not be in our system yet."

"So how do I find out where I'm calling?"

"Sir, why don't you dial the number and ask them?"

I realized it wasn't such a bad idea, and dialed. On the third ring, someone picked up but didn't say anything. After a pregnant pause I ventured, "Hello?"

A muffled voice said, "Yes?"

"I saw this number on a bathroom wall and I wondered about the area code. Who am I calling?"

"Who is this?" The voice was a man's, stilted and overenunciated.

"A friend."

"I think you *c*have the wrong numb*urr*."

I knew who was on the other end of the line. "I'm a friend of Conrad's. You might notice I'm calling from his house. Did you know he's dead?"

"Yes."

"Then maybe you want what he had."

There was a long pause. "What."

"Late twentieth century, oil on canvas, very exclusive artist. One of a kind."

"You don't *c*have anything."

"If it's not for you I have another interested party. Do you want to know more or don't you?"

"I need proof."

"You'll get it. Is this a cell phone?"

"Yes."

"Be at the corner of Grant and Washington at noon. Wait in front of the Kowloon Restaurant. I'll call you." I hung up, grabbed the painting and the bottle, and bolted out the door. I had to get some sleep.

24

By the time I got home, cleaned up the worst of Conrad's bloodstains in my foyer, hopped in the shower, and dragged myself to bed, I was too keyed up and exhausted to sleep. I sat up and put away half a pack of cigarettes and god knows how much whiskey, and slept only a few fitful hours.

Al woke me up. "David?"

"How you feeling, kid?"

"Still sore, but I'm out."

"Still feel like playing backup for me?"

"Yeah. Definitely."

"I'm thinking five o'clock, near the Ferry Building, if everything goes well. Why don't you get a shower and a nap and call me later to confirm."

"I'll go to Vallejo. Hey, is my car still at your place?"

"Still there."

"Okay. Call you later."

I was almost grateful to be hungover. I felt sharper, more focused on the task at hand, less prone to distraction by errant thoughts that might run amok.

I got both my guns and all the ammo I had in the house. I found my old Polaroid camera in the back of my garage and snapped a shot of the post office painting. I took Delores, and I took the tracer. Let them know that I'm not at home.

I left the car at a garage in the Mission, caught the BART downtown, and walked up into Chinatown. I was early.

At a quarter to twelve I was at the window of Ashley's favorite spot, looking out at variegated rooftops and the sparkling bay, enjoying a plum wine as my smiling Chinese benefactress watched over me.

I spotted him right away. He stuck out like a sore thumb, the only sharkskin suit in a sea of hoodies and windbreakers. He lurked in front of the Kowloon Restaurant.

I picked up my cell phone and dialed.

"Yes?"

"On the wall, just near the corner. Do you see the Chinese advertisements stuck to the wall?"

I watched him look around and find them. "Yes, I see them."

"Yellow paper. One large Chinese character."

"Yes."

"Take it down."

Stuck to the back of the ad was the Polaroid.

"Yes . . ." he whispered, seething through the line.

You bastard, I was thinking. *You killed Dalton, you killed Conrad, who was probably working for you, and you tried to kill Alan. And I bet you killed Susan too.* I choked it back. "Are you interested?"

"I'm interested."

"Five o'clock. Near the Embarcadero, across from the Ferry Building. There's a big fountain, wood sculpture. Just sit down somewhere and read the paper."

I hung up and checked the time; I needed to go shopping.

* * *

I met Al in front of the Ferry Building, the streets crowded with end-of-day commuters and tourists, and told him the plan. I had already dropped the painting off with a street artist at the end of Market, and asked him to hold onto it for my friend—in a sharkskin suit—to pick up in a half hour or so. He was so impressed with it that he was happy to have it sitting on an easel in front of his own work—weak impressionistic San Francisco skylines. I handed Al a backpack with my .45. The last thing I wanted was to have him shoot someone in broad daylight, but I felt bad about turning his Colt over to the cops. I still had my Derringer strapped to my ankle. My brand-new Kevlar vest was itchy.

"Don't shoot anyone, okay, kid?"

"Hey, I was lucky the last time. I don't want to go to jail."

"Just sit across from us and keep a lookout for anything out of the ordinary—he might come with friends. If you see me point at anyone, check them—and hard. And if I put my hand on the back of my head, get out of here. Listen, I don't want any cowboy shit. All I want is to walk away."

"Check."

At noon I saw Sharkskin stride into the wide, flat part of the fountain block, look around, and hesitantly perch on a bench, pulling a folded newspaper out of his jacket pocket. He practically glittered in the low brightness of dusk. This guy needed a wardrobe expansion.

I walked right up. He looked up over his paper. "David Crane."

"So you know me," I said.

"Your reputation is . . . known to me."

"Somehow I'm not surprised. Actually, we met once."

"Yes, at the gallery."

"Who do you work for?"

"I'm not prepared to tell you that."

"Where's Ashley?"

"No one knows this. I want to find her more than you do."

I started to get the creeping feeling that it wasn't going well. If this evil bastard wouldn't tell me anything, the silly painting I was holding as collateral would become worthless in a hurry. The fact that Al was keeping an eye on me offered little consolation.

"It is foolish," he said, "that you bargain for information. You should have asked for money, Mr. Crane. You might have got it."

"What can I say? I'm an information broker."

"Information I cannot give. Even if you tortured me, you would get nothing. I cannot tell you where Ashley is." He picked his words carefully, as if negotiating a path through a minefield. "I cannot tell you who she is. And I cannot tell you who I work for, or what it is that I do."

"I sort of had the idea that you kill people."

He smiled.

"Sorry to waste your time," I said. "I can't give anything if you have nothing to offer me."

"That is not true," he replied, tossing his paper aside. "I will leave here with the painting, or you will die. Your decision."

"You're going to kill me right here?" I looked around. It was rush hour; there were people everywhere.

"Look up, Mr. Crane. The tall buildings? Men with rifles. I walk away with nothing in my hand, they shoot you dead."

"You're bluffing."

"Are you certain?"

I didn't think Kevlar would stop a bullet from a long-range rifle, and I didn't want to find out. "But you don't want me dead."

"Would you bet your life on that?"

"You've had plenty of opportunity to kill me already."

He showed me his palms. "I hoped we could keep you alive for one more mission, but I think now this is impossible. I should have killed you last night. But . . . give me the painting, maybe you can live a little while longer."

I had nothing. The only chance was to give him the painting and try to follow him—and try to stay in one piece. I gave the signal for Al to get lost. "Just around this corner," I told Sharkskin, "you'll see an artist selling paintings. He's expecting you."

"Very well." He stood up and gave a preposterous wave as if to call off the snipers. I was sure he was bluffing. I started walking away but he stopped me. "No, no, Mr. Crane." He was grinning maniacally. "You come with me."

I had no choice, and Al was nowhere in sight. I led Sharkskin to where my street artist was guarding the portrait. The artist smiled when he saw me.

"This your friend?"

"Sure," I said, "why not."

Sharkskin took the painting and held it up. "She is talented, don't you think?"

"Yeah. Too good," I said. "Someone should probably kill her."

The artist laughed. Sharkskin was busy holding the painting up to the light, letting the orange sun shine across the canvas, searching for something that I knew he wouldn't find. Suddenly he snapped, held the painting at waist level, and ran his fingers over the uneven area of paint—the tiny depression left by the removed flash drive. He was bursting with rage and spit at me through a clenched mouth: "You stupid, stupid man. You think you can fool me? You think I care if you live or die?"

He lashed out, swinging wildly and knocking over the artist's easel. "Hey, man—" he protested, but Sharkskin revealed a shoulder holster under his jacket, and the artist shut up and legged it. Sharkskin pulled out his gun—sure enough, it was the 9mm Baby Glock—keeping it low and partly concealed by his jacket. He leveled his gaze at me. "Tell me where it is or you die here."

"If you kill me, you'll never find it."

"If you're dead, it can't help you."

And with that, Al appeared out of nowhere and tackled him, just a fraction of a second after Sharkskin squeezed off a shot.

A sledgehammer hit me in the rib cage and I went down, hard. The searing, blinding pain gave way to more searing, blinding pain, and when I was finally able to sit up I saw Al standing over Sharkskin, his nose bloodied and his gun kicked out of reach. Al was pointing my .45 at Sharkskin's head—in broad daylight, in the middle of Market Street. Not good.

"Hey!" A cop appeared half a block away and started

toward us, talking into his walkie. Then I heard the sirens.

"Itchy! Get up!" Al yelled.

I got up off the ground and yelled back at him: "Get out of here!"

Al dove into a passing cab with more grace and agility than I would have thought possible for a man his size.

I ran out into traffic to put a little bit of distance between me and the Shark, who, I was certain, was right on my ass. I dodged a couple of vehicles and a streetcar, jumped back onto the sidewalk, and dashed to the end of the block at full tilt, sidestepping pedestrians. I saw a 14-Mission just closing its doors, with a cop standing next to it, staring right at me. I stopped in my tracks. The cop turned away from me, looked into the bus, and smiled. The doors reopened, and the cop got on. I couldn't believe it, but I hustled and climbed in behind him.

"Hi, Tasha," the cop said to the driver, almost singsong. He was obviously sweet on her. He stood next to her and chatted her up as we rolled down Market.

The bus was crowded, but I managed to get a seat toward the front and tried to catch my breath and loosened the vest. I was sore, and my rib was badly bruised, but I didn't think it was cracked.

The bus stopped, and right on cue, Sharkskin got on. He took a seat right in front of me and turned around, feverish with anger. His nose hadn't stopped bleeding and he was dabbing at it with a handkerchief. "When I first saw you at the gallery," he spoke through clenched teeth, "how I wanted to kill you."

"You keep saying that."

"But I knew you would lead me to her."

I knew it, then. He would kill us both as soon as he had the chance.

"*La próxima vez*"—he made a gun with his fingers and pulled the trigger—"in the head."

"Try it now. Headless man, bus full of screaming passengers—maybe the cop won't notice." I gave up my seat to an older woman and moved a few feet away, hoping he wouldn't start firing at random. The bus was getting more crowded at every stop.

As we approached Powell, I stretched my arms a little, telegraphing that I was ready to get off. Sharkskin stood up and positioned himself right in front of me, fingering the gun in his holster. He wasn't letting me go anywhere.

I smiled at him and watched carefully as we approached the bus stop. I looked at the driver, and I watched the curb, trying to calculate exactly when she would tap the brake. I reached back, all the way back to my ancestors, and when the driver hit the brakes I drove my fist into the back of Sharkskin's neck as hard as I could. The braking of the bus helped destabilize his footing, and my punch put him down.

A woman near us shrieked, "Oh my god!"

I yelled over her, drowning her out, "Somebody help!" The cop looked back, bewildered. "I think he's having a seizure!" I bent down over him, blocking the spectators' view with my body, pasted him in the face, and tried to get his gun out of his holster. He fended me off, one arm tight across the gun. He swiped at me, but his face was a mess of blood and he could barely see.

The cop was already pushing his way toward us. "Here!" I called out. "Please help him!"

I pushed my way to the back door, bolted off the bus, and ran down into the Powell BART station.

25

I rode down to the Mission and retrieved Delores from the garage. I cut through the Castro and took Divisadero all the way north, went through the Presidio and across the Golden Gate Bridge. The view was stunning and I didn't care. I called the precinct and asked for Inspector Willits.

"Yeah."

"It's David Crane."

"Oh, it's David Crane. So nice to hear from you."

"Listen, someone just tried to kill me at the Embarcadero. I think he's on his way to my house."

"Someone's trying to kill him." He wasn't talking to me. "That's too bad, Dave, I'm sorry to hear that."

"I want to come in."

"Yeah, that's not gonna be possible." He was enjoying this. "See, we had a little visit this morning from a couple of agents."

"Agents?"

"Agents. That's what they call operatives of the Central Intelligence Agency."

My heart was in my throat. "You're fucking with me."

"Nope. Two spooks came in and took all the evidence, kicked our dicks off the case, said they'd take it from here." He laughed.

"What's funny about that?"

"It pissed Berrera off something awful. He hates working on a case and having it taken away from him."

"Is that Crane?" Berrera, muffled, in the background. "Tell him we'll see him at the inquest—maybe." They both laughed. I hung up.

I pulled into a gas station in Mill Valley and spied a Volvo station wagon parked with the windows rolled down. I pulled alongside it and tossed my car's tracker into the back. Let Sharkskin chase geese.

I was back on the bridge when my cell phone rang.

"Itchy, you make it?" It was Al, from a pay phone.

"I'm fine, Al. The coppers get you?"

"I rolled out of a moving cab and made it to the BART. They didn't catch me."

"Good for you. Lay low, Al. Stay out of it and watch your ass."

"What are you gonna do?"

"I'm going to find out who's pulling the strings in this puppet show."

I went back to the deer blind. If Sharkskin couldn't be bribed, perhaps one of his underlings could be threatened. My surveillance, Ashley's paintings, Conrad's operation, Sharkskin's string of murders—everything led to the deer blind. And to one skinny, pizza-loving sentry.

I parked at the Shell station and made straight for the back house, holding a pizza box and wearing a crappy baseball cap. I knocked loudly. Through the French doors I saw my friend's shadow bobbing to the door. He opened it slightly and poked his head out.

"Pepperoni, extra cheese?"

He blinked. "I didn't . . . I didn't call . . ."

"Whattaya mean, you didn't call? I got a pepperoni, extra cheese here."

He looked from side to side, unsure how to manage the situation, wondering how I had found him and weighing it against his favorite pizza. It was all I needed.

I flipped the pizza box into the door and shoved it, knocking him back as I stepped in and came at him with the tire iron I'd hidden under the box. I caught him haphazardly under the chin. He fell against the wall and I hit him in the head to be sure, then quickly shut the door and locked it behind me. I turned off the lights and went to work on the kid with a roll of duct tape—wrists, ankles, mouth.

The blinking green light of the tracer from my car was just off the 101, near Novato. The monitors showed my empty house. The audio recorders were still, only occasionally rendering the waveform of a passing car on my block. No one knew where I was.

I sat down at what looked like the main computer and sniffed around, finding the e-mail program. Most of the incoming and outgoing e-mails were in Spanish, and more detailed than my language skills could decipher. They seemed to concern the movements of someone named "Balam," and were largely just notes—like the minutes from a meeting or an ongoing journal. The incoming messages were short, direct, and full of words I didn't recognize—code, perhaps, or just slang.

Then I saw a name I recognized: *McCaffrey*. I clicked the top of the page to organize incoming mail by sender and this revealed a long list of correspondence from McCaffrey—going back months. He was involved, he knew these people, he was part of the conspiracy to bury me.

So why would he hire me to find Ashley?

I heard something and turned around quickly, just in time to see a blur coming toward me. There was a dull thud and a ringing, and I spun backward into blackness and knew nothing but the sinking, inky dark of the void.

"**B**alam *viene aqui?*"
"*Sí, veinte minutos, más o menos. Se fue de la casa de Eechy.*"

"*Entonces?*"

"*No sé. Qué quiere.*"

"*Pues.*"

"*Mira—sus ojos son abiertos.*"

They both looked at me and I realized I was looking at them. I felt like I had been run over by a garbage truck. The skinny one was holding ice to his head, and I was jealous. The big one, the older one, the one who had obviously knocked me out, was grinning. He came over.

"Do you want to see my favorite movie?" He turned to his friend. "Carlos, *la película de* Balam *y el gordo.*"

Carlos put his hands on a computer and clicked away. The big one rolled me over in front of the monitors. The bastards had me taped to a rolling office chair—with my own duct tape. It was covering my mouth as well.

Carlos pressed play and stepped out of the way so I could see. The big one loomed over me. It was a tape from my house, time-coded and date-stamped. It was today, maybe a half hour after I had arrived at the deer blind—recent, though I had no idea what time it was now. My house was still, empty.

There was the sound of the front door opening violently and Al fell into the living room, followed by Sharkskin. He moved Al to the couch by waving a gun—a .45 automatic. My gun.

Sharkskin looked away from Al and started to yell. Carlos adjusted the volume so we could hear him. "David Crane! *Está aquí o no?*"

Al looked scared. "I tole you he wasn't here."

"But you don't want to tell me where he is."

"I tole you—I don't know where he is. I called him—all he said is he wanted to find out who was in charge."

"And where is the girl?"

"I don't know anything about—"

Sharkskin yelled into the house again: "*Dónde está la cucharita!*" Then he snarled at Al: "Where is the little slut?"

"I don't know nothing about the girl. David didn't even know where she was."

"Not good enough, fat one. Not good enough." He steadied the gun on him and Al visibly squirmed.

"I tole you what I know—I can't tell you where he is if I don't know."

Sharkskin seemed to think it over. Then a phone rang. Sharkskin reached into his piscine jacket and pulled out a cell phone. "*Hola.*" He listened. "*Verdad? Muy bien. Perfecto.*" He hung up, put the phone away, and looked at Al. "*Qué suerte* . . . you are very lucky, fat one. You have no problem. I know where Itchy is now. You have no problems, no problems anymore."

Then he shot Al three times in the face. I tried to look away but the big one held my face toward the screen, laughing. Sharkskin put my gun on the coffee table and peeled off his latex gloves. Al would be discovered, dead in my house, killed with my gun. Poor bastard. Sharkskin looked up to the camera and spoke in a steady voice: "That was almost more fun than killing your girlfriend." There was a sound of sirens in the distance and he made his exit.

Carlos was clapping his hands. "*Qué incredible*, Balam!" They both fell into laughter again as I shut my eyes tight. I almost didn't hear it in the background—"South San Francisco Police, freeze!"—and another muffled pop. My eyes flew open and I saw my empty house, Al dead on the floor, the sound of a car screeching away from the curb. Michael. It was Michael's voice—the cop, my friend from across the street. He must have heard the shots and caught the killer coming out. I shut my eyes, tight as I could. Al's dead, and so is Michael.

"*Voy a fumar*," the big one said, and I felt him brush by me and I opened my eyes to see Carlos busying himself at the machines. I realized they had neglected to tape up my ankles. I could feel a flash of cold on the inside of my right ankle, just above my sock—my little Derringer, still strapped where I'd put it before meeting Sharkskin—Balam—at the Embarcadero. This was doable. If it weren't for the tribal drum circle in my head.

Something about the feeling was almost familiar. I felt slow and sluggish, as if every nerve ending in my body were clogged with peanut butter. I was a little nauseous, worsened by the thought of two decent men dead for nothing, and had a screaming headache. I knew this feeling, I just couldn't quite put a name to it.

I felt hungover. *La goma*. That was it. The aftereffects of a falling-down, shit-faced drunk. I know how to function hungover: move slowly and watch out for gravity.

I raised my leg gingerly and Carlos didn't turn around. I brought my right foot up and over to my right hand, gripping the cuff of my trousers and pulling the pants leg up. I lifted my leg higher and brought it over to my left hand, brought my ankle in a little closer. My left thumb found the butt and braced it; my index finger found the trigger. I tried to line up. I couldn't get a high shot, but I might be able to tag him in the leg. I slumped, drunkenly, farther into the chair, twisted the gun as high as I could in the belt, guessed, and squeezed.

Carlos and I both started howling at once. The heat from the shot burned my ankle with scalding pain. I hit him. I didn't know where, but I hit him. He grabbed at himself and fell onto the floor, curled up and screaming bloody murder.

I stood up, taking the chair with me. The big one was back inside and coming at me, yelling, *"Maldito relamido de verga!"* I spun the chair around and caught him in the gut with the chair's wheels as he lunged toward me. His breath rushed out of his lungs. I tried to swing the chair again with my ass and took a quick punch to the face—I heard my nose break, felt the blood gushing down my lips and chin—then ducked just enough to miss the full force of the fast-following second hit, which glanced across my eyebrow.

I crouched down and forward, pushing into a jump, and drove my head into his chest. He fell back. Carlos, still howling, tried to come at me and I kicked him in the face. He went back down, moaning and spitting teeth. I slammed the chair into the wall—once, twice, three times—pulling at my right arm. The big one was up and hit me in the stomach, then again in the mouth.

My right arm popped free of the tape. I hit him in the face and forced him back, hands slipping—there seemed to be blood everywhere. He had my tire iron now and was coming back at me—the chair was still taped to my left arm and I swung it at him, gained a second, got my Derringer from my ankle, and squeezed off the other shot. This time he stayed down.

I didn't know how close Balam was and I wasn't anxious to see him. I wrestled the rest of the duct tape off of me and started unplugging wires. I freed up the two hard drives and pulled them out from under the console, grabbed one in each hand, and stumbled out the door, ignoring the whimpers and moans from the two bleeding men.

It was already dark and the streetlights made me squint, my vision like a screech in my head, materializing in the actual sound of sirens whining in the distance. Gunshots in a quiet suburban neighborhood. *Time to go.* I lurched as quickly as I could to my convertible, threw the hard drives in the backseat, wiped some of the blood out of my eyes, and started driving.

27

I set the hard drives down and banged on the door—
my shoulder banged back.

"Hang on!" Rider called out. I leaned on the jamb;
my arm was half-wrenched out of its socket. Rider was
taking his sweet time getting downstairs. I saw a fleck of
red and stepped back. I was leaking, leaving paint splatters
on his porch. Cadmium red, maybe, or alizarin crimson.

The door finally opened and Rider's eyes nearly
popped right through his wire-rimmed glasses. "Holy
shit! Itchy, what happened to you?"

He took me in and put me in the shower. I made it a
cold one, and then spent some time in the mirror investigating the damage. My face was a mess. My nose was
visibly broken, leaning to one side, and my lip was swollen to twice its normal size and still oozing thick, dark
blood. I had a goose egg on my head, giving me an ele-
phant man profile. I looked like hell, but I was still alive.

I met Sobczyk in the kitchen and he handed me a
sandwich. "So it *is* the CIA."

"Apparently. They kicked the SFPD off the case, and
I doubt anyone's looking for my Guatemalan. And he's
looking for me."

"Everyone always thinks I'm paranoid." Sobczyk
blinked hard, twice. "Did you find the girl?"

"No."

"You think she's dead already?"

"Can't say."

"It would be pretty lame if she died after trying to save you."

"Yeah, Sobczyk." He couldn't have put it better. "It would be pretty lame." I took a bite out of the sandwich, wincing with my swollen lip. "More dead."

"What?"

My mouth was full. "I mean if she got *more* dead. She's already officially dead. She got accidentally put on the Death Master File."

Sobczyk blinked again. I didn't think it was possible for him to look more serious than usual, but he did. "You didn't tell me that."

"I forgot."

"That's on purpose," he said. "No accident."

"I don't think so."

"Too many coincidences tend to equal a conspiracy," he said. "Someone put her on that list."

I kept chewing.

Sobczyk shook his head. "If you want to find her, it's got to be an ex-boyfriend," he said, wiping down the counter. "I mean, if she's alive."

"Is that what all the good conspiracy books say?"

"No, man, that's just always the way it is on TV. The convict always ends up at his ex-girlfriend's place."

"That's TV."

"Ostensibly, TV is based on reality. That many cop shows wouldn't be in agreement for nothing."

"You have a point, I guess. But I checked the ex-boyfriend. Nothing. Let's see what Rider's got."

Rider had the hard drives from the deer blind

propped up on a stack of magazines and was working two keyboards and two monitors—one for each drive. "In terms of surveillance, you don't have that much here," he said. "They were purging files on a regular basis, looks like every day."

"You mean erasing the footage?" I asked.

"If they were recording you twenty-four seven and keeping it all," Sobcyck said, "you'd have a lot more of these drives."

"Yeah," Rider agreed. "Right here. Yup. Dumped. Daily. But we do have the last . . . let's see . . . eighteen hours, since the last dump. Which means we have this." He brought up the clip he had just watched of Sharkskin and Al in my living room.

"Don't," I said. "I've seen it already."

Rider took it down. "I'm just telling you, you've got proof. You got the guy, you got a fucking murder on tape. And he confesses to another—*your girlfriend?*"

"Susan Dalton. What about the e-mails?"

"Man," Rider said, taking off his glasses and wiping them on his T-shirt, "it would take some time to go through all of this. Most of them are in Spanish, and I'm sure most of them are just inter-office whatever, if you know what I mean. I looked at some of the notes from your pal McCaffrey, and if the rest is anything like that, it's mostly crap. Scheduling, paychecks, errands—I mean, if you didn't know better, he could be the manager of a Pizza Hut. Same day-to-day bullshit."

"Nothing explicit? Nothing about either of the Daltons?"

"Itchy," Rider said, "I've only been alone with these for half an hour."

"Sorry, I know. You're the best. Both of you guys."

"What next? What can we do?"

"Can you copy all of that?"

"I've got a spare drive," Sobczyk said. "How much data is it?"

"Not that much, really," Rider answered, kicking one of the drives. "This one is mostly porn."

"All right. Make a copy of everything pertinent, and bury it. Keep it someplace safe. Then take the originals to the cops."

"I thought you said the cops wouldn't help," Rider said.

"Go to the Northern Police Station, on Fillmore and Golden Gate, and ask for Inspector Berrera. He's kind of an asshole, but I think he actually gives a shit. Him or his partner, Willits. You tell them you have a video of a guy getting shot at Itchy Crane's house, and they'll listen. Tell them what I told you—that there's a guy running around town killing people, that he's probably an operative or somehow sanctioned by the CIA. Get them to take it to the FBI."

"Berrera and Willits?"

"Yeah. And give them my apologies. Sobczyk, can I borrow some clothes?"

"Sure."

"Rider, can I borrow your car for a few days?" He made a face. "Look, give me your car, and I promise that when all this blows over, I'll let you borrow mine."

"Seriously? Dude, you're gonna let me drive Delores?"

"I can't be seen in that thing. After I got my face rearranged, I left it in long-term parking at SFO and took a cab here. I'll let you pick it up when this is over."

"Oh, man—let me get my keys."

It was high time I checked in with McCaffrey.

28

Rider had an old Honda Civic. Nothing fancy, not too beat up, backseat full of fast-food detritus, and excellent gas mileage considering what I was used to. I drove as if possessed and made LA in record time. McCaffrey's office building was on 4th, near the 3rd Street Promenade. It was still the middle of the night, so I found a parking garage, moved into the passenger seat, and passed out.

I woke up midmorning, the sunlight heating Rider's Honda to oven-level temperatures. Every part of my body felt like it had been run over. I fell out of the car and tried to stretch, cracking my back audibly. I pissed in the lot, leaning on the hood heavily. It was now or never. I loaded up my little Derringer and walked over to McCaffrey's office. The lobby was a typical high-ceilinged, polished-interior nightmare, and the bored security guard gave me a startled look when he saw my busted-up face. I grinned, shrugged, and he didn't bother me. I checked the list on the wall for McCaffrey's agency: sixth floor.

The elevator was mirrored and I looked away. The office itself was white and minimalist. McCaffrey's secretary sat at an alabaster island in the middle of a waiting room with chairs that seemed straight out of *Star Trek*. She looked as bored, as blond, and as tragically washed out as she had sounded on the phone.

"Can I help you?"

"I'm here to see McCaffrey. He's expecting me."

"Your name?"

"Conrad Johanssen. But don't tell him who it is. He thinks I'm dead."

She gave me a blank stare, blinked, and picked up the phone.

"Mr. McCaffrey, I have a Mr. Johanssen here. He says that you think he's dead . . . ?"

She pointed at the hallway behind her. "Thanks," I said, and headed back, worrying the gun in my jacket pocket. The door to McCaffrey's office was open, and he got out of his chair as I entered.

"Itchy," he said, smiling, "I thought that had to be you." He hadn't changed. His paunch was still prominent, his thinning hair still bleached blond, his ugly face still beaming with rancor. He still favored overpriced suits, but wore only a T-shirt underneath, a look that should have died in Miami in the eighties. He crossed the floor with a hand extended. "Damn, you look like hell."

I kicked the door closed behind me, stepped to him, took his hand with both of mine, pumped it once, smiling, and on the upswing stepped around him and caught him in an arm lock, pulling and twisting his arm away from his body in a direction it was not designed to go. He grunted.

"Don't scream, McCaffrey." I fished the gun out, kept him bent in front of me, put the gun to his temple. "Not a fucking sound."

"Uh. You wouldn't."

"Try me."

"S-sit down. Talk this over."

"Who's setting me up?"

"Wait—wait—"

I pulled his arm a little harder. He flinched. "Who's setting me up, McCaffrey? Why did you want me to find Ashley?"

"Stop it, please."

"Answer me."

"Itchy, come on . . ."

I leaned in so close he could feel my breath. "Who. Is. Ashley."

"She's my daughter."

"Bullshit."

"She's my stepdaughter."

I yanked his arm and he squealed. I wasn't buying that either.

"She's my ex-stepdaughter. Fuck, I'm like her uncle."

That got me. I let go but kept the gun on him. "Sit down. In *front* of the desk." He did. I sat on his desk across from him. "You smoke in here?"

He was rubbing his shoulder. "I quit."

"How LA of you." I took out a cigarette and lit it. "Speak."

"Why do they call you Itchy anyway?"

"What?"

"Why do they call you Itchy?" McCaffrey seemed suddenly calm, almost sincere. "If you're going to kill me, I want to know."

"I got that at the *Chronicle*. I was such a drunk that by midday I'd be twitching and scratching myself." I shrugged. "Don't be so convinced I'm going to kill you.

I might just shoot you in the kneecaps. Tell me about Ashley."

He let out a long, depleted sigh. "I was married to her mom before she died. Look, that kid never had anyone. Dad died young, mom was a bum—hot, a stripper, and I think she hooked too. When I met her she was trying to clean up, working at Disneyland, if you can imagine that. Living in Anaheim and working at Disneyland. It's like . . ." He trailed off.

"White trash in a rich suburb."

"Exactly. I was married to her less than two years. Ash and I got along. She was obsessed with the private dick business, wanted to learn everything. It was fun having her around. Cute kid, y'know? Maybe thirteen, smart as hell. I used to let her take pictures of people trying to defraud insurance companies. Y'know, guy with a back injury, you catch him loading cinder blocks. She was great at watching people. Decent photographer too—always had a good eye. Me and her mom split up, the mom latched onto some other poor schmuck and they moved to San Francisco. I didn't hear from Ash after that."

"Until she disappeared?"

He reslicked his thinning hair back with the flat of his hand and wiped a bit of spittle from the corner of his mouth. "You're not going to like this."

"I haven't liked any of it."

He rubbed his wrist and looked me in the eye for the first time. "A couple years ago, the mother of one of Ash's old middle-school friends in Anaheim comes knocking on my door. Rich bitch, totally Orange County. Her daughter was killed up in San Francisco. The cops closed the case, would I look into it? Something about a nude beach." He read the cloud passing over my face. "Do you remember her name, Itchy?"

"The girl's name was Patty. Her boyfriend was . . ." I couldn't bring it up.

"Patty's name was in all the papers, but no one remembers the name of the boyfriend who died on that nude beach. You know why? It was a pretty white girl from Orange County dating a black guy from Oakland. And they weren't lost, they were wasted. There was nothing wrong with your directions, Itchy—they were both drunk and stoned out of their gourds. Patty's mom kept that out of the press. She wanted someone to punish, and the boyfriend was already dead. His parents live in the Acorn projects—West Oakland—there was nothing to gain by going after them. So I went digging and found you. Hired you to help me on some—I don't remember."

"A gravesite search in Colma. Your irony was intact."

"Got me a closer look at you."

"You threw me under the bus."

"I gave Patty's mom a scapegoat. This job isn't about learning the truth, Crane, it's giving people what they pay for."

"You killed my career. Why shouldn't I kill you right now?"

"Please. The Internet had your number. Besides, you're not a killer, Crane, and you're not an information broker. You're an information *junkie*. You want the story."

"Who the fuck are you working for, McCaffrey? And don't tell me Ashley's dead friend's mom."

He looked almost stung. "I never wanted to get into this. Business was slow. I was tired of staring though binoculars at some fat-ass fucking his mistress. I was approached by . . . an organization."

"Come on."

"I don't know what else to call it. They do consignment work for the CIA."

"What kind of work?"

"They kill people, Itchy, all right? They kill people. They do what the CIA isn't technically supposed to do anymore. They kill bad people. Or that's how it was pitched to me. They needed boots on the ground—reconnaissance, surveillance, information management. I find out things they need to know, I manage a small group of guys who keep track of potential targets. Someone else does the dirty work."

"And you set up a patsy to take the fall for the hits."

"Yes." He looked at the carpet. "I guess you know just about everything."

"Not quite. How did Ashley get into this?"

"When I went up to San Fran to investigate the nude beach, I tracked her down, found out her mom had been dead for a few years—"

"How did she die?"

"Lung cancer. No foul play, just bad luck, and a two-pack-a-day habit for decades. Ash had been living on her own since she was fifteen. Squatter communities, artist communes, co-ops. Real counterculture shit, man. She lived at the old Dolores Street Baptist Church—the one that burned down. Camped in Golden Gate Park. It's a tough town to be homeless in, but the kid still finished high school. When I found her she was answering phones at Macy's, just turned eighteen, ready to start her life. And then she found out she was dead."

"The Death Master File."

"Fucking 'keystroke error.'" He winced. "She was just eighteen, it was terrible. She hadn't had a fixed address in years, she didn't have any ID, she could barely prove she was alive—she couldn't build anything. She needed help." That stung look again. "I got her an apartment, kept an eye on her. Gave her a job."

"In your criminal organization."

He flinched, blood pressure spiking. "It was just a part-time job to help support her painting." He ran a hand across his hair again and took a deep breath. "Nothing dangerous, no big deal—little fill-in jobs. One of the jobs was you. Watching you, logging your movements . . . the tedious grunt work of a routine surveillance case. That's all it looked like, that's all she knew. She liked it, and she was good at it. Then she started to have some kind of a thing for you."

I let that go. "She worked at the house in San Mateo?"

"When we set up shop there. Look, it's not like we've been watching you twenty-four seven for two years. We'd set up an observation post, and when the job was done we'd take it down."

"And Ashley watched me get framed for three murders."

He threw his hands up. "There was you. There was Ash. And everything just kind of clicked. We were looking for a new subject, and the Bay Area was a leading contingency. No one would miss you, no one would cry for you. And after the nude beach, maybe people would think you had it coming. Besides," he raised his shoulders and let them down again, "you fit the profile."

"Excuse me?"

"You're white, you're of a certain age, you have no family. You have your own business and you work alone. You have few friends, fewer girlfriends. You own guns, you're a good shot. You have a history of depression and alcohol addiction."

"And I have motive to kill people I've never met?"

"With your prints on the murder weapon and no alibi, no prosecutor would worry too much about motive. They'd make a case for you as a lone gunman, a misfit, a serial killer. If it came to that."

"Meaning?"

"It's coverage, Itchy. There was never any plan to turn you in to the cops unless there was a hitch. If we smelled heat, we'd put them on you. A fall guy, for emergency use only. It wouldn't even matter if the charges didn't stick—by the time anyone figured anything out, we'd be long gone."

"And that's worth the expense of keeping tabs on me."

"It's not as expensive as you'd think. Besides, if you learn one thing as a subcontractor for the government, it's to keep your expenses high. As soon as you save them a little money they slash your budget." He pulled at his T-shirt collar. He sounded calm, but he was sweating. "Look, I don't have anything against you, personally. In a perfect world all the jobs would've finished clean and you'd never have known anything about this."

"I don't find that reassuring. Since when does the CIA kill people in the United States? What happened to foreign dictators?"

"The CIA has their fingers in every pie, people in every region. And people from other countries come here. It's not always easy to get to a target. They play a waiting game, lining up targets with opportunity. We'd only planned three jobs on you, then you'd be done."

"Three jobs. Martiartu, Natali, and Rodgers."

"Wow." McCaffrey shook his head. "You really are good."

"Save it."

"Yeah, the Cuban was the first one. Hard guy to find—kept changing his name. The Agency had been looking for Martiartu since Bay of Pigs. And the Natali thing . . . that had been in the works for a long time too. Tran—the gangster in the Tenderloin?—was connected to bigger fish in Asia. The Agency was shutting Tran down on two continents, and Natali knew too much to let him walk around."

"But some random young guy sitting in his car in Oakland?"

"I know. That was fishy from the get-go. I didn't know who he was. I don't even know if the guy they killed was actually Lucius Rodgers. We were told to get THIS guy, matching THIS description, at THIS address. They told us less than usual, and it was last minute. That's why we brought in Balam—we'd never used him before, and I didn't like it."

"He didn't kill Martiartu or Natali?"

"No, no. Martiartu was a lifer who works South America and the Caribbean. He knew Martiatu's background—might have known him personally. Natali . . . the guy who did that job is dead now. Afghanistan."

"Sad story. So if all three kills came off without a

hitch, I should have been done. What happened?"

"Balam happened." McCaffrey shook his head. "He did the Rodgers job. We planned to keep an eye on you for a couple more weeks until we were sure the cops had nothing. Then we'd shut it all down, I'd get a fat bonus, we'd pull the gear out of your house, done. But Balam was hanging out with the *chapines* in San Mateo."

"*Chapines?*"

"Guatemalans. The guys I had working at the shop. They got all buddy-buddy. And Balam met Ash and didn't trust her. She always had her drawing pad with her, sketching you, and he thought she should be . . . contained. No one ever noticed her before—her 'art' seemed harmless enough. Or so we thought." He put his hand to his forehead and went silent. "Give me a cigarette." I lit him up, and he exhaled a cloud of smoke toward the ceiling. "After the Rodgers job, he noticed a flash drive missing. They're brand new, practically prototypes. Balam was convinced that she'd stolen one, and he turned her studio upside down and found stuff."

"What stuff?"

"I don't know. He said he had proof that she'd been copying files from your jobs. But Ashley must have known he was on to her—she disappeared. And Balam started calling shots—pushing Conrad around, trying to find Ashley and anything she could have used to move data."

"Her paintings."

"Exactly. And I had one. She sent it to me. The one I sent to you. I was looking at it here, in the office, and . . ." He fell off. "They were gonna clip her, Itchy. They didn't want to talk, they were just gonna kill her." He stamped the half-smoked cigarette out on his desk, bending and breaking it, spilling tobacco flecks. He put his hands over his eyes. "I just wanted to save her. That's why I called you."

"You know I'm under surveillance, and you hire me?"

"I tried, all right? I called for a data purge the day I contacted you. Everything shuts down during a purge—recording, the feed, everything. No one was watching or listening when we talked."

"You called me the day Dalton got whacked."

"Did it again. I was afraid Balam had killed you already. When you picked up I figured Balam was setting you up for Dalton too. That didn't come from me."

"He knew I was looking for her. I used my home phone to call the Dalton Gallery—how did you think I could find her without anyone noticing?"

He threw up his hands. "I did what I could. You don't know the risk I took. I would've been killed too—because of the flash drives. I was DEAD. Me and Ash both. You were the best person to find her. They wanted you alive—"

"I don't like that I was responsible for leading a killer to the Daltons."

"Conrad already knew about the painting at the Dalton Gallery. Whether Dalton was an arranged hit or not, who cares? It's a fucking free-for-all now. Balam? He's insane. He's completely off the reservation. Susan Dalton? She was less of a threat than her brother. And Conrad—fuck. I can't believe he killed Conrad."

"He thought Conrad would talk."

"You tipped off the Bigfoot chick at the gun range?"

I nodded. "Conrad let something slip."

"I had Conrad under control. He was ruthless, but

not psychotic. Look—the outside assets got their marching orders from the same people I did. Middlemen, talking to the Agency with one side of their face. I don't know who the directives came from. Balam and I were peers, get it? I can't say he wasn't getting orders that conflicted with mine."

"You didn't know who you were working for?"

"It's Black Ops, Itchy. The less you know, the better. Indirectly, we were all working for the CIA. And Balam—and hit men in general—came from a guy they call the Old Man."

I perked up. "The Old Man?"

"It's bullshit. Some creepy Hassan-i Sabbah reference. I don't know the guy."

I did. Or, at least, Conrad did.

"Where are the guns, McCaffrey? I'm going to need them."

He sighed. "They're here." He got up and went behind his desk, turned the dial on a floor safe. He handed me a package: three guns, all in Ziploc bags. "The three hits. Wipe them for prints first." They were dated in black Sharpie, like something you'd put in the freezer.

"Where's the other one?"

He slipped another bagged gun out of the top drawer, laid it on the desk, and sat back down. It was a 9mm Glock.

"This isn't it."

"Isn't what?"

"This isn't the last gun they took off of me."

"What the fuck are you talking about? There were three guns on you—that's it."

"There were four. Charlie confirmed they picked up a gun from her on the day Dalton got killed at the gallery—

but I knew it couldn't have been used for that hit. And Conrad said they were keeping me alive for another job. What other job?"

McCaffrey shook his head. "There was no other job. What else did he say?"

I shrugged. "He said a lot of shit. He asked if you hired me. What is this gun?"

"That's what Balam used to kill both Daltons. It doesn't have your prints on it, but he sent it down thinking we could plant it in your house."

"Think, McCaffrey. He already planted it on you."

"What? They need me," he said, but he was giving it thought.

I looked at the 9mm. "If he got my prints on another gun, maybe he could preserve them and use it later to kill someone else."

"Maybe you're not remembering it right, or Balam lied to me. Maybe your prints *are* on that gun."

"No. The gun I shot was a Baby Glock—a subcompact. Balam still has it, I saw it. I'm not an expert, but this is maybe a Glock 19—" I stopped when I saw his face; he'd gone whiter than his office walls.

"I kept it in the floor safe." He sounded far away. "When I couldn't find it . . . I thought I'd taken it home, drunk. But I couldn't find it there either."

"The Baby Glock was yours?"

McCaffrey leaned forward in the chair, almost keening. His voice went to a whimper. "It's me. It's obvious. Balam must have put it together. I was scheduled to go to San Francisco today to close Balam out. That would have been my funeral."

"Why didn't you?"

"Because you shot up my guys in San Mateo. Stole the hard drives. I've been on the phone nonstop doing damage control."

"You think Balam's on his way here?"

"No. He's a ghost. Someone else will come for me."

"You said Balam was crazy."

"He's not stupid. He's been made. My guys are in the hospital, in custody. Balam is on a plane, I'm sure. Probably back in Guate by now."

I walked behind the desk. "You got something here?"

"Bottom left."

I found the bottle and poured us a couple of stiff ones. We drank without toasting.

"So," I asked, "where are we?"

He laughed. "We're dead, that's where we are."

I finished my drink and put the glass down. "Get your toothbrush, McCaffrey. I'm taking you in."

"Do I have a choice?"

"Afraid not. The FBI has already heard about this little fiasco, and I need you to vouch for it. Everyone else is dead."

"They can't protect me, Itchy. The FBI—protective custody, whatever. I'm a dead man, I promise you."

"Let's hope you're wrong."

"Itchy." He looked exhausted. The very breath was sucked out of him. "Where is Ashley?"

"I didn't find her."

"Damnit." He pushed his hair back so hard I expected what was left of it to come off in his hand.

"At least she's alive, McCaffrey. If she weren't, we'd know about it by now."

It was a long, quiet drive to San Francisco.

29

I took the 580 off the 5 and jogged over to the San Mateo Bridge, the long thin pencil spanning laterally across the bay, so unattractive compared to the iconic bridges of the City. I got on the 101 and quickly blew by my exit, watching Sign Hill roll by—*SOUTH SAN FRANCISCO, THE INDUSTRIAL CITY*—and then we were at Brisbane. I always do my best thinking driving across the causeway at Brisbane—my bay, my personal piece of the ocean.

I'd missed it. The question wasn't why Sharkskin didn't clip me when he had the chance, it was why the organization didn't clip Ashley long before she gummed up the works.

I looked at McCaffrey, petulant in the passenger seat of Rider's Honda. He had hired me to find her. Despite all his evil deeds, he didn't want her dead. He'd put me on the case knowing I was connected to it, knowing that sooner or later I'd loop back to him if I weren't killed in the process. And he'd saved me the red herring— Ashley's last name. McCaffrey had blacked it out on her driver's license when he sent it to me. It wouldn't have helped me find her—she didn't use it anymore. But if I'd been a little smarter, I would have gone straight to McCaffrey when I found her name and realized she was "dead."

I was off the highway and climbing up Fell Street

when it occurred to me how close the police station was to Rider and Sobczyk's place. Instead of turning onto Fillmore I went on to Scott, then turned back down Hayes and pulled over at the corner of Alamo Square Park. Even through Rider's dirty windshield, the view was sickeningly cute. The park, the Painted Ladies—the neat row of Victorian homes as tidy as a film backdrop—and the City's skyline sharp in the distance.

McCaffrey looked at me. He didn't know where we were, what was happening.

Sobczyk's voice rang in my head: *Someone put her on that list.*

I turned the car off and spoke very softly: "Who put Ashley Fenn on the Death Master File?"

He didn't say anything. His face was turned to the window, and he brought a hand to his brow. I swatted the hand away and punched him in the head. It bounced off the window and I hit him again.

"Who put Ashley on the Death Master File?" I was yelling now.

"I don't know."

I hit him again. A woman pushing a baby carriage squealed and hurried past. I didn't give a fuck—*Call the cops, we're headed to them anyway.* "It was you—I want to hear you say it." I hit him one more time and his head on the window sang like a ripe melon.

"I didn't—I didn't—"

"Why'd you put her on the list, McCaffrey?" I reached for my Derringer. "I'm gonna put one in your fucking leg—why'd you put her on the list?"

"No," he whimpered, growing smaller in the seat. "I did it, I did it . . ."

"Why?"

"I'm an idiot, I fucked up."

"You fucked up, but you're not an idiot. You did it on purpose. Tell me why."

"I needed someone I could trust."

"Like she trusted *you*?"

"It was a big promotion, it was the chance to get in on something big. I don't speak Spanish, the crew I had—like Conrad? He'd sell me out for nothin'—"

"You 'killed' your own stepdaughter for a fucking promotion?"

"I couldn't lose her after losing Patty!" he yelled.

I was in shock. "Patty . . . ?"

"Patty, goddamnit." He was half-crying, half-spitting, punching the dash. "The girl who died on the nude beach. She was my fucking daughter."

I heard the words almost before he said them. How could I miss something like that?

"You never could've known," he said, as if in response. "Her mom and I were young, we had broken up, I wasn't gonna do the right thing—she put *Ronald McDonald* on the birth certificate just to spite me. We did a paternity test—she was mine, all right—and she made me pay support but cut me out of her life. But years later, when I'm with Ash's mom, Ash is in seventh grade and she brings home a new friend. It's Patty." His eyes lit up. "It happened so organically her bitch mom couldn't say shit. I had a daughter. We got close—even after she moved to San Francisco. And Chris was a good guy!" He glared at me. "Her boyfriend—they were good together. But her mother couldn't stand that he was black, and when they died she wanted someone to lynch. I knew it

wasn't you, Itchy. Just . . . what? Two kids in their twenties, smoking reefer and drinking beer on the beach? In
California? You never—you don't think . . ."

He fell apart, and I felt bad for him in spite of everything. I remembered what Conrad had said just before
he bought it—I had wrongly assumed he was talking
about Ashley: *Do you even know about McCaffrey and the girl?*

"I can see how this put you back onto Ashley," I felt
almost guilty saying it, "but the Death Master File?"

He put his hand over his face and started shaking.
He was crying, but there was no liquid coming out—he
was all dried up inside. I put the gun in my jacket. "She
wouldn't work with me," he said, through choking sobs.
"I offered her everything—a place to live, a job—but she
wouldn't come along. She said I abandoned her and her
mother, that she was better off on her own. It isn't true.
Her mom left ME. And Ash . . . I wanted her back. I
wanted us to work together like the old days. And . . .
if she had nothing else . . . we could help each other."

I just looked at him. It was so deeply fucked up, yet
completely opportunistic—the sine qua non of McCaffrey's being.

"It was supposed to be a moment in time," he said,
looking up at me. "Like a bankruptcy. This day, dead,
then, tomorrow, back alive. But I couldn't turn it off.
After I gave them her Social Security number—it was
over. The system is too complex, and the octopus . . .
too many arms . . ."

I called Willits—with McCaffrey bawling in the
background—to let him know we were coming in. Willits was animated; he had an FBI agent with him, Sob-

czyk and Rider were at the station, and they were all trying to piece it together. But I couldn't find a parking spot. I made the block—Fillmore, Turk, Steiner, Golden Gate—three times and finally gave up. I pulled up and double-parked in front of the station, got out, and called over a uniformed officer.

"Can you watch this guy? He's a suspect in a murder case—I can't find a parking space. I just need to get Inspector Willits or Berrera."

"All right. Be quick."

I leaned in the window to McCaffrey. "Just sit tight. Don't do anything stupid."

"They can't protect me, Itchy." He seemed resigned. "They can't."

"We're at a police station, McCaffrey. Relax."

"Hey, Itchy?"

"Yeah?"

"I'm sorry." He gave me an almost wistful look. "You're a better man than I thought. Of all the men she's had to meet . . . at least she fell for you."

"I'll be right back."

It was minutes later when I came out with Willits. He sent the uniform on his way and gave me directions to a parking lot, then opened the door of Rider's Honda.

"Mr. McCaffrey?"

It took us almost a full minute to realize he was dead.

Cyanide. Old-school spook shit. McCaffrey must have really believed he'd never make it, and took the easy way out.

I was held for close to seventy-two hours. Willits and Berrera took my statement before I was cross-examined by a hard-ass FBI agent named Siegel—midforties, square-jawed, classless, no-name suit, *Dragnet* all the way. I was back and forth between a holding cell and an interrogation room as the interested parties determined my fate. I never did ascertain how much the FBI already knew about the CIA's involvement with Balam's "organization" or how much they believed me. Suffice it to say that the FBI and the CIA don't talk to each other very much.

Eventually I was released. There wasn't anything to charge me with. The two guys I shot had disappeared—an unidentified "agent" of some kind had walked them out of the hospital in front of at least a dozen cops. They were either dead or ghosts. I wasn't a flight risk, so the FBI let me walk provided I kept myself available for further questioning, and Willits, who seemed to forgive my previous petulance, promised to keep me in the loop.

My side of the story held up, despite the fact that no one was left alive to corroborate it. The 9mm Glock from McCaffrey's office matched ballistics to the deaths of both Daltons. My .45, of course, killed Al, and with the corroborating evidence of the surveillance of Al's murder, it was taken at face value that the man on the tape in the sharkskin suit had killed both Daltons as well. Not that anyone would ever see him again. Conrad's killing still couldn't be proved without a murder weapon, but overall the authorities were buying the "single killer" theory. Meanwhile, the ballistics lab was busy trying to match the guns McCaffrey had given me with the three unsolved murders he and I had discussed. Again, no one would ever be charged, so I wondered how much it mattered.

Sobczyk and Rider gave me a lift home with one of their weird friends—a surveillance specialist—and gutted my house. While they were working I took a cab to SFO to pick up Delores, and went over to Kaiser and had my nose rebroken. It would look and feel bad for some time, but at least it wouldn't be crooked forever. When I got home, the boys had pulled so much crap out of my house they were giddy as teenagers.

I wandered around my house, seeing it as if for the first time. Here I'd been, thinking I was all alone in an obscure corner of the world, when a rogue's gallery had been watching my every move.

I had a nice chunk of change now, from McCaffrey's initial 25k, and if I could bury the guilt over the deaths of Susan Dalton and Michael and Al, I could resume my quiet life in South San Francisco. Sleep late, eat big breakfasts, take afternoon naps.

But Ash was still out there. She'd fallen for me, or thought she had, hard enough to paint portraits of me, to assemble my alibis, to risk her life for me. Sure, I'd been nursing a quiet, unresolved fantasy about her ever since I saw her picture at Masello's place—I am a man, I'm not blind. But it had evolved past that. I had feelings. West Coast, oogy feelings that I didn't want to talk about. It haunted me that the bastard McCaffrey could be responsible for so much of what happened to Ash . . . and yet be the one who put us together. It felt fated.

Besides, how could I trust McCaffrey with anything? Where was Balam, really? And how many other people were working for the "organization," communicating with Conrad or the Old Man or whoever, unbeknownst to McCaffrey? Would Ashley be the next to wind up dead? Maybe on a nude beach somewhere, just to twist the knife?

I slept like the dead in my own bed, like a brick laid by a master and smothered in mortar. As the sun split through my back window and the birds started up their morning racket, I nosed halfway out of sleep, then ducked halfway back and saw something, an image shimmering in front of me, lit in sharp contrast, like something hung in a gallery.

It was a painting—by Ashley, of course. But this one was different—it wasn't an event that had already occurred. It was a variation on a theme, an almost exact replica of the painting that I had discovered in the cocktail lounge in Chinatown. Me, caressing a lover. Only the lover was Ashley.

It was truly beautiful. *She* was truly beautiful. And the look on her face . . . she was so much in love. I hovered before it, overcome with an emotion I had no name for.

There was a small tear at the corner of the canvas and I gave it a pull, and as it ripped the hole grew and spilled audio tape, reels and reels of it. I tried to patch it with pieces of canvas but realized the painting was changing, ripping, turning into something else—

I woke with a start and a sharp inhalation of breath. I remembered the lead I had never followed up. I never asked the Elvis Costello look-alike at Pearl Paint about Ashley's disappearance.

I had to find Ash. I had to see her with my own eyes.

30

I had slept late. Afternoon was well underway by the time I got to Market Street between 5th and 6th. He was easy to find. Masello was right—he really did resemble Elvis Costello. Tall, gangly, glasses, and a quirky demeanor.

"Can I help you?"

"I want to ask about a customer of yours. A woman named Ashley who had an account here?"

"Oh, yes, Ashley. What a knockout. Typically we don't run tabs for individual artists—accounts are more for commercial accounts or contractors—but for Ashley I made an exception. I had a little crush on her."

"Has she been in lately?"

"No. She closed out her account, hasn't come back. Couple weeks ago."

I did a double take. "A couple of weeks ago?"

"Yeah. Two, maybe three."

I wandered off in a daze, almost forgetting to thank the guy. Jason Masello told me that Ashley disappeared a few weeks before I talked to him. But if she paid the tab two or three weeks ago, then she had barely been missing from the neighborhood when I talked to Masello. Maybe Sobczyk had a point when he said that it was always an ex.

I drove to the house on Hill Street and saw a note on the door: *Babe—at the Lone Palm. J.*

I knew the place, right around the corner on 22nd, steps from Guerrero, next door to a bodega that had gotten some press for making a giant ball out of rubber bands. Pink neon screamed *Lone Palm* next to a martini glass over the awning. I ducked in. The afternoon light struggled through a lone window, the bar, stools, and cocktail tables bright enough to dispel the myth the joint perpetrated in the evenings—that it was dark enough to be swanky and not just another Mission District hipster watering hole. The tables were covered with white tablecloths, the candles already lit. The television above the corner of the bar played some old black-and-white Tarzan movie with Maureen O'Sullivan, as if to intensify the noirish vibe of the room.

I took a look around and spotted Masello in the back corner, near the restrooms, hunched over a draft beer, his face flickering as he laughed and whispered to his chubby lady.

"Masello." I sat down without being invited.

"Oh, uh, hi. David, right?"

"That's right."

"This is my girlfriend, Dana."

I shook her limp hand. She looked past me, half in the bag.

"Cut the crap, Masello," I said, quietly but firmly. "Where is Ashley?"

"Oh jeez," he whined. "I'm so over this. I told you, I don't know."

"You don't have to protect her anymore."

"What the fuck." He looked at Dana and rolled his eyes theatrically. "I don't know where she is."

"Masello, it's done. Her uncle is dead—"

"Her uncle's dead?" Dana's eyes were as wide as gla-
ciers, fixed to me. Both Masello and I stared at her.

"Dana," Masello said, "what is it?"

She shook her head. "Oh, she's going to be so upset."

It was a small studio on Potrero Hill. Dana had rented
it for Ashley and brought groceries over every couple
of days. They had met while Ashley and Masello were
dating and liked each other. After Dana and Masello got
together, she and Ashley stayed in touch, no animosity.
When Ashley went underground, she went to Dana. Ash
knew Masello could never keep his mouth shut, and she
knew that no one would ever ask Dana. Who expects a
guy's girlfriend to cover for his ex? Only in San Francisco.

Dana had a key and let me in. I asked them to allow
me to go up alone, and they stepped aside. I climbed
the staircase trepidatiously, nervous in a way I hadn't
felt since high school. I reached the top of the stairs and
turned into the tiny space, a small room cluttered with
painting paraphernalia. There were several easels set
up and it was hard to see if anyone was even there. It
sounds strange, but I felt her presence in the room. Buried beneath the smells of paint and lacquer thinner was
a subtle, fragrant scent that I couldn't quite place, but
that I wanted to lie back and smell for a year or two.

I followed my nose to an easel set up by the back window, a half-obscured view of the tiny backyard next door
with a garden—birds of paradise and a Meyer lemon tree—
and the subtle backdrop of Potrero Hill falling away.
The light was gentle and buttery and caressed the easel; a palette leaned against it on the floor, littered with
clumps of drying pigment. A pair of brushes crossed on

the ledge of the easel—this was clearly the canvas she had been working on. It was Delores, my convertible, driving down what looked like Lombard Street, and the unfinished woman riding shotgun looked just like Ash.

"She's not here," Dana said, at the door, a wringing worry in her voice.

I touched the edge of the canvas and burnt sienna came off easily onto my fingers. "It's still wet."

"She promised me she wouldn't go out," Dana said. "She even said it was too dangerous."

Masello was sobering quickly, his look shifting from shock to concern. "Why would she go out? If it's so dangerous for her—where would she even go?"

It was obvious. She was a woman of passions, and a creature of habit. "I know where she is."

31

She wasn't there. It was almost happy hour, yet the Empress of China was deserted. I asked for a cocktail menu and took a club chair against the wall facing the bar. It was foggy over the bay, the top of Coit Tower smudged into invisibility. Then I saw it: on a table by the window, an unattended drink. Looked like plum wine.

It sounds strange, but I felt her come into the room. The second I heard the elevator door open, I knew it was her, returning from the restrooms downstairs. She drifted by me and I caught a whiff of what I had smelled in the studio, a scent of amber, with a top note of what might have been acetate from her studio and a woodsy base with a hint of musk.

Masello's photograph didn't do her justice. She was stunning. Everything about her emanated beauty. This was the kind of girl who made heads turn everywhere she went. This was the kind of girl who could make a rowdy Mexico City barroom fall silent at her mere appearance at the door. She wore a big baggy sweater that gave the top half of her body a formless shape, and tight black leggings that defined what little of her legs weren't covered by the sweater. Her thick socks were pulled up high above beat-up Doc Martens. Her hair was cropped short and swept up off her neck in some trashy kind of kerchief. She was dressed for a Saturday, a stay-at-home, never-leave-the-house, mop-the-floor kind of day. It didn't matter. A girl like that would be stunning in rags. Her face simply beamed radiance. I almost fell onto the floor.

She moved effortlessly to the north window, taking her seat like an empress, and after a sip of wine she sat staring out the window and didn't move.

Well, this was it. I hiked up my ego and sauntered over, feeling like a clumsy teenager. I clenched the back of the chair opposite her to keep from carrying on right through the plate glass.

She didn't look up.

I sat down.

She didn't look up.

I waited.

She didn't look up. Every essence of her being was captivated with the scene out the window—the bay, the Golden Gate, and Chinatown laid out before us like a specimen awaiting dissection. Her eyes reflected the blue tranquility of the ocean itself. She was utterly at peace; one could never have guessed that her life was in such danger, that people had killed and died looking for her. She was beyond it all. I could have been Jack the Ripper and I don't think she'd have minded.

I couldn't take it anymore. I spoke: "Ashley."

She slowly turned her head until her eyes landed on me. I felt like I'd been hit by a rock. She registered no surprise at all, just enthusiastic recognition quickly followed by excitement. The smile that broke across her face threatened to spill into her drink or float up to the ceiling. She came out of her seat and toward me, hugging me to her and pulling me up as well, until we were both standing, clumsily.

"David." Voice like a waterfall over evergreens. "I love you."

I was speechless. She squeezed me tight for what felt like an eternity, then sat back down and pulled me with her. She looked at me across the table with pupils as big as dinner plates and reached out to touch my face. "You have two black eyes," she said, and laughed, with a sheer joy that was almost tangible. It was true, the broken nose had left me raccoon-eyed. "I love you," she said again. I didn't know whether to kiss her right there or blow my brains out.

I had to say something. I'm a man. "I don't know you."

"I know. But I know you very well."

"I still don't understand. Any of it. How can you love me?"

"I watched your tapes." The smile was a man killer. "I saw you sleeping, even. I listened to your phone calls. I know everything about you."

That's when the invasion-of-privacy instinct is supposed to kick in. It didn't. "The tapes . . ." I was floundering. I could only repeat her.

"The tapes from your house, silly." I rather liked her calling me silly. It made me think we were naked in a lagoon far from guns and thugs. "From the cameras in your house." She flushed a little and giggled.

"And the letter? That was really from you?"

She nodded. "I wanted you to know I was okay. I knew I shouldn't, but—I didn't want you to worry."

Worry about someone I didn't yet know? "Why didn't you tell me about the cameras?"

"They couldn't think anything was different." She dropped the smile for the first time and I was able to slightly relax.

I really wished I had a whiskey. Here she was, right in front of me, and I didn't have the foggiest notion of what to do next, what to ask, where to go, how to get there. All I could think about was taking her somewhere. Alone. Like Big Sur, or Kauai.

"Listen," I said, "I'm sorry to tell you . . . your, um, 'uncle,' McCaffrey—"

"He's dead, isn't he?"

"Yeah."

She shrugged. "He knew it was coming."

"I'm sorry—"

"Fuck him." It was harsher than the words themselves, cold coming out of her. "He was the closest thing I ever had to a father, and I never heard a word from him, not even after my mom died. Then he shows up, years later, wants me to come to work for him. Because of *David Crane*"—she bent her voice into an imitation of McCaffrey, full of ire. "*He's a bad guy. He got your best friend killed. You have to help me.*"

"You mean Patty. The nude beach."

"Whatever." That shrug again. "We were friends for a minute in middle school—it's sad that she died, but . . . did you hear about Typhoon Winnie?"

I blinked. "You mean last month, in Asia?"

She nodded. "*That* was tragic. Patty was just sad."

"Did you know she was his daughter?"

"Yes. He tried to make up for not being around when she was younger, probably. Forgot about me until she was dead." She took a sip of her wine. "She replaced me when we were younger, and now he wanted me to replace her. He was all desperate-like. I said no. I had a new job at Macy's. I had a tiny room in a big apartment, I had a boyfriend. I had an art show coming up. And then everything went away, because I was 'dead.'"

"And then you had no choice."

"I had a choice," she snapped. "You always have a choice. I would have survived just the same. But I was basically kidnapped."

"What?"

"The goon squad. *Live* here, *work* here, *we're following you twenty-four hours a day. For your own safety.*"

I was confused. "I thought you went to work for him willingly."

"Never."

"Ashley, McCaffrey is the one who put you in the Death Master File."

"Oh, I know. I could see it in his stinky eyeball. But someone didn't like it. I was taken care of after that." She smiled. "And then I saw the *bad guy*. The guy who killed my friend Patty. Only he didn't kill anybody. And he wasn't a bad guy. And I thought, *I can do this for a while.* David," she leaned in, her eyes wide, "it was a *nice* apartment. Money for paint and canvases. And everyone shut up around me. I don't know why."

A waitress appeared and I ordered a whiskey.

Ashley smiled at me and tapped my shoulder playfully. "Don't look so creeped out," she said, and then, "Look how beautiful it is," looking out the window. She was right, it was, and we were quiet until the whiskey came. Even though it came in an uncomfortable snifter,

I put down half of it in a single slug. I felt ebullient for a second.

"Can we get out of here?" I asked. "Get out of town, you and me?"

She smiled so big I thought Coit Tower would bend to its gravity. "I'd love to," she said. My heart beat. "Where is Balam?"

That broke the dream into a million little pieces of sharp, blinding reality. "I don't know. McCaffrey thought he'd left the country."

"He could still be coming after me."

"I don't think so. McCaffrey's guys are gone, the whole operation is blown. No one's watching me." She was shaking her head. "Look, Balam wanted you dead because you were stealing files and flash drives to protect me. Now that—"

She was laughing, head back, mouth wide open. "I wish!" That got the waitress's attention and Ash didn't skip a beat, just ordered another wine from halfway across the room with a single gesture. Then she quieted down. "Balam was obsessed with me. That's it, the end."

"You mean, like—"

"He wanted to *fuck* me. Marry me. Own me."

Balam's cudgel-like face rose up in my mind.

"I only ever saw the boys at the shop, no one else. They were fun, silly boys. But when Balam came, he knew them from before, and it was, *Hola, chapines, vamos a ver*, whatever, talking garbage. And Balam came on to me. I was like, *No*. But he kept coming by. He said he loved me. *As if*." She looked back out the window, pensive.

"Ash," I said quietly, "what then?"

She chewed her lip. "He came to my studio when I wasn't there. He didn't find any flash drives. I was *careful*. He found my paintings. Of you. He flipped out. He knew I was in love with you and he went crazy."

I remembered the quiet fire behind Balam's eyes, even the first time I saw him at the Dalton Gallery.

"He said he'd kill me if I didn't have sex with him." She pushed it off, the way you'd brush off a harmless insect. "It wasn't that. I've had sex with guys for worse reasons. Whatever. But . . ." She stared at me, her eyes glistening. "I knew I wanted you. I didn't want anyone else and I wasn't going to do anything for that . . . *fucking psycho*." She spat the words, her face twisting into a mask of disgust. "Balam said he'd kill us both. He knew I wanted to help you, and he told his bosses that he had hard evidence. But he was guessing. Carlos tipped me off. I think he had a little crush on me." She grinned. "Then I had to disappear. He could kill *me*," she said, taking my hand, "but he wasn't going to kill you."

I just looked at her, dumbfounded. Her hand was cool in mine and calming.

"Kiss me," she said.

Her face was serene, with its own gravitational pull. I leaned in for a kiss that would make every other kiss I'd ever had in my life seem paltry and pale, a kiss that would cut to my bones and make me blissful, calm—stupid.

And then the room erupted in chaos. Half a dozen FBI agents in blue windbreakers stormed the room, brandishing guns and yelling. I saw Siegel's face and stood up. Two agents grabbed me and I saw Ash being forced out of the room. "The Old Man!" she was yelling at me. "*The Old Man!*"

And my angel, my demon, the source of all my troubles and the source of my salvation, was gone like the last tendril of smoke from a stamped-out cigarette.

32

"So are you boys staying at the Holiday Inn Chinatown?" I asked. "You know that's the one with the pool on the roof from *Dirty Harry*."

"Don't hate me, Crane, I'm just doing my job," Siegel said, not taking any bait. I was back in an interrogation room.

"And a hell of a job, Siegel. Can't even find a little girl without tailing a washed-up journalist." I hated him, all right. Finally being in a room with Ashley had burned her image into my retinas—every time I opened my eyes I expected to see her, and this prick was in my way.

"We knew you weren't telling us everything."

"I told you what I knew, what I thought was relevant. What do you want with Ashley anyway?"

"She's our only connection to McCaffrey and the organization he collaborated with. We need to debrief her, and keep her in protective custody."

"Protective custody? You didn't even know where she was until I led you to her. Come to think of it, no one's been able to find her except me. Not McCaffrey, not Balam, not the FBI. What is this bullshit?"

Siegel tapped a pen on the table impatiently. "What is it you want, Crane?"

"I want to see her."

"Can't allow it. I have to know what she knows, and I can't have you influencing her."

"So you're keeping her sequestered." I was ready to knock him out. "It's funny, Siegel, you say you're protecting her, but you don't seem too bothered about me walking around, living in the same house, driving the same car—what makes you think no one's coming to kill me?"

"Nothing in your statement indicated that anyone was ever trying to kill you. But Ashley—"

"And the shot I took in the chest? If it weren't for Kevlar I wouldn't be here."

"I understand your frustration, Mr. Crane, but you explicitly stated that McCaffrey's people wanted Ashley dead. We don't want that to happen."

"Bullshit. You want to pick her brain."

"If we had McCaffrey in custody it would be a different story."

"Don't put that on me. If you had met me outside the police station he wouldn't have had the time to eat cyanide."

Siegel made a face like he smelled something foul. "McCaffrey didn't take cyanide. That's just the official report."

"What?"

"Small pimple-like entry wound at the back of his neck. They're still isolating the toxin."

"What, ricin? You're telling me they gave him the Georgi Markov umbrella gun while he was sitting in front of a Johnny station?"

Siegel nodded. "The outside cameras were switched off the minute you pulled up. We've got no record of what happened outside. It wasn't ricin, it wouldn't have acted that fast, but yes. We believe McCaffrey was murdered."

"Shit." I didn't know what else to say. The Old Man's people must have improvised. "So when can I see her?"

"When she's finished telling us what she knows, and we're reasonably certain no one else is coming for her—"

"How would you know?"

He let that go. "We can't keep her against her will unless she's charged, and I can't imagine she'll be charged with anything. Eventually, she'll be released on her own recognizance." He cleared his throat. He was leaving something out.

"Eventually?"

He didn't say anything.

"Siegel, tell me what I'm missing."

He gave me a long, steely look and didn't seem to breathe for what felt like a full minute. Finally he blinked. "She's not cooperating."

I laughed, long and hard. "I love it. Did she say why?"

"Because of you."

I was still laughing and it obviously irritated the hell out of him. "But you won't let me see her."

"It's against protocol. Crane, she thinks you're still in danger. She doesn't want to give us anything until she knows you're safe."

"Maybe she's right—maybe I am still in danger."

"What was the threat to you other than Balam?"

"Do I need another threat? No one knows where he is."

Siegel's poker face went awry.

"*You* know."

"No," he said firmly. "But we know where he's not. I—this is classified, Mr. Crane."

"Everything is classified. I can fix Ashley's cooperation problem if you cooperate with me."

He sighed and tapped his pen a few more times. "Balam met his CIA handler at SFO. She was waiting for him with a ticket out of the country."

"So you know where he went."

"No." He didn't say anything else.

I was losing what little patience I had left. "I have all day, Siegel. You?"

He put his pen down. "He killed his handler. Shot her dead in the long-term parking lot. He never got on the plane."

"So he could be anywhere."

"Not anywhere. Based on our intelligence, and what little the CIA has shared with us, he likely crossed the border into Tijuana, and will turn up in either Mexico City or Guatemala City."

"And your boys will pick him up."

"Ours, or the CIA's. Their agents are working in cooperation with ours."

"You believe that?"

"No. I think they want him dead."

"No shit. I guess you want him alive."

"We'd like to talk to him. But your point is valid—if he gets killed by his own people we can close the books on Ashley. We can wrap up this tentacle of their operation. Obviously, if we get Balam alive there are more possibilities."

It was all bullshit. These guys wouldn't find Balam, and even if they did, it wouldn't help anyone. McCaffrey

had known he'd never get away from the organization—
Balam would know that too. He'd never be taken alive.
It was naïve to think they had forgotten about me and
Ashley. The job wasn't done, it was blown, and someone
would want the mess cleaned up.

I remembered what Ashley had screamed while they
were dragging her away from me, and how agonizingly
close we'd been just moments before.

"You with us, Crane?" Siegel prompted me.

"Yeah," I said. There was only one place to go, and it
wasn't Mexico or Guatemala City; it was an address on
a mailing tube for a painting of Ashley's that never got
delivered. "If I can find Balam, will the Bureau leave us
both alone?"

"Of course. Don't expect a congressional medal of
honor."

"Promise me that if Ashley tells you everything she
knows, you'll let her go."

"We can't keep her."

"Let me talk to her."

He stroked his chin, blinked, and picked up the
phone. "Put her on." He cupped his hand over the phone
and handed it to me. "There are people listening."

"There always are." I took the phone. "Hello?"

"Hi, David." I'd recognize that honeyed voice anywhere. It almost took my breath away.

"Hi." I felt suddenly awkward with Siegel watching
me. "Listen, Ashley, do you trust me?"

"I do."

"Just tell the feds whatever they want to know, and
they'll let you go."

"And then I will see you."

"Of course."

"You know where to go?"

"I do."

"You can leave messages for me in Chinatown, David. I'll find you."

"I have to go."

"I love you."

"Right back atcha, kiddo."

I hung up, and noticed Siegel glaring at me. "That's it?" The phone rang and he picked it up. "Siegel. Okay, I'll be right there." He hung up. "She's talking."

"Can I go?"

"Yes."

"Should I expect the FBI to keep following me everywhere I go?"

"No. And we won't be looking after you, either, so watch your step."

I got up to leave.

"Thanks for your help, Mr. Crane."

"Fuck you, Siegel."

GUATEMALA

I booked a flight to Guatemala City via Houston and bought a couple of books to read on the way. Filling in the holes of what Sobczyk had told me about Guatemala didn't make me any more comfortable.

Since the early 1900s, United Fruit owned the town of Puerto Barrios and all of its port facilities—it was the only Atlantic port in the country—as well as the rail lines, giving the company almost complete control over Guatemala's international commerce. It paid no taxes until Árbenz came into power. It was no wonder he had to go. When Armas was instated, he gave United Fruit all its land back and abolished the tax on interest and dividends to foreign investors. He also jailed thousands of political critics.

But his honeymoon didn't last, either. After barely three years he was implicated in bribery scandals and, ultimately, shot dead in the street. His assassin was found dead too—an apparent suicide. Rumors abounded that the hit was called by one military officer or another, or by American mobsters, since Armas had been harassing casinos—shades of JFK and Havana—or by Dominican Republic dictator Rafael Trujillo. The truth never came out.

Nobody won. Almost as soon as Árbenz resigned, the Justice Department sued United Fruit for violation of American antitrust laws. It lost ownership of the railroads, sold off its land holdings to Del Monte, and merged with a conglomerate called United Brands. By the seventies, the empire was disintegrating and the corporate president, Eli Black, smashed a hole in the quarter-inch-thick window of his New York Pan Am Building office and jumped. After his death, investigations concluded that during his presidency, United Brands had bribed European officials as well as the president of Honduras. With the company now facing charges from a federal grand jury, whatever was left of United Fruit's legacy passed on to Chiquita Banana and Dole.

It seemed that everyone touched by the CIA's Guatemalan coup met strange ends. John Peurifoy, the US ambassador to Guatemala during the coup, was killed in a car crash in 1955. Frank Wisner, one of the CIA's deputy directors and a Black Ops expert who had helped engineer the coup, committed suicide. Jacobo Árbenz, the deposed president himself, drowned in a bathtub in Mexico in 1971. His favorite daughter, Arabella, shot herself in Bogota in front of her boyfriend at the age of twenty-five.

I knew I had to be crazy. I would probably get myself killed. But fuck the feds, fuck the CIA, I was bringing Balam back and I was going to make a life with this girl.

The stewardess tapped me and asked me to raise my seat for landing. I put my books away and realized that the snack we'd been served was still on my tray table—a plastic tub of yogurt and a fresh yellow banana. It was funny to think that no one in the United States had ever eaten a banana before 1870. *Bananas*, I thought, as we flew low over the outskirts of Guatemala City and green foliage passed under us, filling in the gaps between low buildings crowded together. All for the sake of bananas.

* * *

On the ground. Off the plane. Through passport control, through customs, cashed a traveler's check for a wad of quetzales. I stepped outside into the broiling Guatemala City sun, a fierce hello accompanied by bustling activity— dazed travelers searching for a ride, locals gathered in anticipation of greeting family members, taxi drivers hustling for a fare.

I walked upstairs, across the parking lot to the street, and waited for the number 83 city bus. I rode in silence, buffeted by activity as people got on and off, chattering in Spanish. I barely looked at the map in my Lonely Planet book, *La Ruta Maya*, the Belize and Yu- catán sections dog-eared, the Guatemala pages fresh as *pan* Bimbo. The bus took us by the zoo, through Zone 8, riding down the long, nightmarish, slow-moving thor- oughfare of Avenida Bolívar, eventually turning off into Zone 1. The rampant dilapidation of Guatemala City . . . on the brink of absolute devastation, a destruction in progress, everything dirty, smog-stained, cluttered. A massive, sprawling experiment in confusion, a contu- sion of modern Western amenities—fast food and auto service stations—and the ancient, tried traditions of a former Central American empire.

I got off the bus, threw my satchel over my shoulder, and started walking in the stultifying heat and oppres- sive pollution. I was relieved to find that Guatemala City has a grid system, with numbered *avenidas* and *calles*, and I easily found my way to the Transportes Litegua bus sta- tion and bought a ticket for the five-hour ride to Puerto Barrios. Not that there was an option—the railroad had long since stopped running. It was a nice bus by local standards, like a Greyhound, with a smelly bathroom on board and little TV screens to show American movies dubbed in Spanish. I slept most of the way.

I woke up just outside Puerto Barrios at a quick stop in front of a mirrored building, like something from the cityscape of Dallas, completely out of place. Next door was a Pollo Campero—a fast-food chicken joint— advertising itself with the image of a cartoon chicken serving up a plate of fried chicken. The scene struck me as slightly ridiculous. Mirrored buildings, chickens serving chicken, and me, the only gringo on a bus bound for a coastal town without a single resort.

I got off at the bus terminal as the sun threatened to sink, making it the hottest part of the day. Two words for Puerto Barrios: hot and dusty. I half-expected to see a tumbleweed sweep through the center of town. I walked, sweating, until I found a *posada* on a side street littered with sparse trees. Anything for a little shade, I thought, and inquired about a room. A middle-aged woman showed me to a tall concrete bunker with a tiny twin bed, a three-pronged ceiling fan with ten years of dust hanging off it, and a private bathroom with a flush toilet but no seat. There were towels that looked almost clean. I dropped my satchel and told the *dueña* that it would do. She nodded and said I could pay later.

"*Hace calor*," I said, as if it weren't obvious.

She laughed, showing silver teeth.

I switched the fan on, swirling with a monotonous rhythm, and remembered Ashley, her voice . . . *Kiss me* . . . the selenography of her face. I fell asleep, dreaming of guns and violence.

I walked out into the evening. The piercing heat had

barely faded; my skin felt sticky in the ambient glare of streetlights, and my eyes chafed in their sockets, so full of dust they gave out an almost audible rasp when I blinked. I found a *comedor* and ordered a *bistec*, and sat on a cheap plastic patio chair at an outdoor table nursing a lukewarm orange Fanta. The steak was cut thin, but was tough as a leather belt and salty. As I ate, the señora wiped down the plastic tablecloths at the adjoining tables with bleach. Somehow the searing aroma only added to the flavor of the experience. I was a long way from home.

I wandered aimlessly. The streets were not exactly empty, but sparsely populated, giving off the anticipatory feeling that anything could happen. This was a place that time had forgotten. The glory that United Fruit built had been lost to the synapses of history. On an otherwise empty block, behind chain-link fencing, a stable of white Dole tractor trailers sat more innocuous than foreboding. The railroad tracks were empty—cold bones to be jumped over playfully by small children and emaciated dogs with sad eyes. The bay itself was a dead-end lagoon, lending a brackish background scent to the town and little more.

I passed a loud roadhouse and ignored the catcalls of the prostitutes standing at the door. "*Hola, guapo, qué pasa?*" I wasn't handsome, I was white. White means money.

I found a bar that clearly catered to tourists and expats and stumbled in for a whiskey. I tried the local—Old Friend—which was slightly more palatable than nail-polish remover. An American tried to make friends by telling me a story about getting robbed in the bar, shouting, "*Ayúdame!*" to the proprietor. Midway through his follow-up tale of contracting dengue fever and being tended to by a local girl, a friend of his came in and he excused himself. I moved from the bar to a back corner and sat alone until an aging black man sat down next to me.

"You are looking for something?"

I wasn't, but we chatted anyway. He was from Livingston, the Garifuna town up the coast, accessible only by boat, on the border of Belize. I told him I was a journalist, working on a story about United Fruit.

"Be careful what you write, my friend," he cautioned, a Caribbean lilt in his voice. "They have long tentacles." He was, of course, referring to El Pulpo, The Octopus, the nefarious company's time-honored nickname.

"You're joking," I said. "United Fruit has been defunct for decades."

"No, no," he wagged a finger at me, "not defunct. They want you to believe it, that is true. But not defunct. They control the land, still. They stop farmers from working their ancestral land—beat them up, drive them away from their farms. Or they put them in jail. And if they give land to the Indians, they give land that is not usable. Land that will not grow a banana, not grow anything. And not just land . . . it is more now."

"More what?"

He looked up into the ceiling. "This is the modern time. There is more money. Not in fruit, in other things. El Pulpo, now they have other businesses. Fruit, yes. And drugs. And cars. And tourism. Where they can find money, they make money. I tell you, wherever you find bad conditions, you will find United Fruit."

I finished my drink. "It's hard to believe."

"Believe it, brother." He fixed me to the wall with a

hard stare, and pointed a gnarled, craggy finger in my face. "Materialism is a fucking spiritual jail."

I went back to my cell and lay for a long time, staring at the ceiling fan.

The Hotel del Norte was a relic, a dilapidated, faded building that utterly failed to convey any of its former glory. Strictly ghost-town, and even the ghosts were on vacation. One had to look closely to imagine the boys' club it had once been.

The grounds included a small courtyard centered by a fountain—not working, half-filled with fecund green water—decorated with fish; an outdoor pool table with faded green felt, covered by a rickety awning; a kiddie pool with a slide, clearly a later addition; and to the side, the main swimming pool, very small, with *Hotel del Norte* inscribed in the bottom. The pool faced the main dining room of the hotel, separated by screened windows and a battered screen door. The old bar was wooden and still beautiful, but made ridiculous by tables topped with red-and-white-checkered plastic tablecloths and cheap plastic chairs.

A plump, middle-aged woman came to the screen door. She smiled sweetly.

"*Qué busca usted?*"

"*Disculpe, estoy buscando el Hombre Viejo.*"

Her smile evaporated, and I wondered if I had come all this way for nothing. Perhaps the Old Man was already dead. The woman shifted her weight, wiped her hands on her apron, and gave me a disquieting look. "*Un momentito,*" she said, and was gone. In a few minutes she reappeared and opened the screen door.

"*Pase adelante.*" She sat me at a table. I felt small and alone in the large, darkened room.

"*Quiere algo a tomar?*"

"*Una* Coca, *por favor.*" It was still early and I was already sweating in the fierce, piercing heat. The woman brought my soda and a cheap tin ashtray and disappeared again.

I sipped my Coke. I brushed off a passing thought that I was about to be killed. It was too hot, and I was too tired to give it much worry. It wasn't long before I was joined by an old man, midsixties, heavyset, and Guatemalan, although with very fair skin. He was wrinkled and paunchy, but carried his girth with an assured importance. He sat down across from me without speaking. I said nothing.

"It was different," he began, his English clear and his voice sturdy, a man who was accustomed to being listened to without needing to raise his voice. "It was different, before, in the old days. Then, we were fighting for our lives, for our livelihood, for our families. Fighting was *normal, regular.* It was the price of doing business. We had to choose a side. On one side, Jacobo Árbenz, and his empty promises of a socialist society. On the other side, United Fruit, who gave us homes, work, money, and the possibility of prosperity. You can see, for a young man, how one could be seduced by such a possibility. When one is young, it is easy to imagine a future. When one becomes old, one realizes that future . . . is an illusion. There is only the memory of a past that, perhaps, did not occur as one remembers. And the now. After now, there is nothing."

I nodded. If there was ever any question that he knew

who I was, it had been erased by his opening speech. It was as though he'd been expecting me. He pulled out a cigar and lit it somberly with a match, took a couple puffs, and laid it in the ashtray.

"After the CIA, after Árbenz was removed . . . another choice. Politics and business, or the other thing. And all was military—you could not be a politician without the military. You could not be in business without the military. And so the other thing became more attractive to many of us. It was the only way to have freedom, to remain on the outside. To work for yourself, to decide, *Today I work, tomorrow I rest.* To be free from politics and business. And there was much work. Yes, we assassinated Castillo Armas in '57. He had become an embarrassment. In the sixties, we were very busy. Frank Wisner, a former friend, in '65. Everyone believed he was a suicide. Before that, in '61, Rafael Trujillo, dictator of the Dominican Republic. Even Congo Prime Minister Patrice Lumumba, the same year. Our first job out of Central America. Eisenhower, Dulles—it was a crazy time, *entiendes?* Your congress investigates, sometimes, and discovers that the CIA is not involved." He laughed, a bruiser's infectious chortle. "Every political assassination in the world in the last fifty years, the CIA was involved. One way or the other, *verdad?*

"In 1971, when Árbenz drowned in his bathtub in DF"—he pronounced it *Day Effay*—"that was one of us, yes, but it was a personal vendetta. His daughter"—he waved his hand—"that was a true suicide. We had nothing to do with that. But the seventies were difficult. El Pulpo was suffering. Eli Black, the company president, he made so much trouble," he chuckled dryly, "we finally had to push him out a window in New York. They called that a suicide also. But the investigation . . . the world was changing, and we needed to expand our business. We could no longer rely on United Fruit, on the politicians who allowed civil war to go on for so very long. We wanted to grow out of Central America, and our connections . . . the Dulles brothers were gone." He picked up his cigar and realized it had gone out. "Do you remember Dan White?"

It was like a shock from another world. "From San Francisco?" I realized it was the first time I had spoken. He nodded. "You were behind Harvey Milk?"

"No." He smiled as if addressing a child. "But we could have. Moscone, that could be good money for us. This was when I realized that we must have more . . . *cómo se dice . . . huellas?*"

"Tracks? Footprints?"

"Like this," he smiled. "We must have more footprints in more places. You see, 1976, your President Ford made illegal any political assassination. But for the CIA, to tell them not to kill is to tell a fish not to breathe water. This is what they know. This is what they are. And we, like them, unable to evolve, to crawl onto dry land and breathe air, we become more removed. One step away. Fish, *todavía*, but fish in a glass aquarium." He relit his cigar, shook out the match, and flicked it to the floor. "This is business. But," he puffed, "only God knows what can become now. When I think of your *paisano*, Michael DeVine, *conoces?* The American murdered here for nothing?" He shook his head. "It makes me sick in my stomach. This kind of behavior . . . the attention it brings . . ." He fell off, tapped his cigar, and left it in the ashtray. "I am boring you. You did not come here for a history lesson. You want to know about Balam."

I finished my Coke and, through a series of hand gestures, he asked if I wanted another and signaled the woman to bring it. While we waited for her return I fumbled for my pack of Rubios—the local cigarettes I had bought that morning—lit one, and said nothing. I wondered why he was being so cordial. It was like a meeting with the Godfather—I couldn't be sure if he was about to grant a favor or bash my head in with a baseball bat.

My fresh Coke sweated on the table as he continued: "Balam's father was a refugee of the civil war. He worked in acupuncture, and he performed it on prisoners of war. But he did terrible things, *entiendes?* To disrupt the flow of chi, all the terrible things you can do to a person—and it appears you are helping them. And so, there becomes a hit on Balam's father and on all his family. They become refugees, they go to Canada. Balam learns English. He becomes strong. But he doesn't like the life, and he returns to Guatemala City. Imagine, in school, with teenagers, there are lockers for guns. The students are permitted to bring their guns to school. Balam's father gives him a gun and tells him, *Look after yourself. I will not pay your ransom.* Because, you see, in the eighties—now, *todavía*—kidnapping is very common in Guatemala. This is a way that people can get money. You kidnap a child, you ask for ransom. If the parents don't pay, maybe you kill the child. Maybe you bury the child alive. This happened many, many times. This is the environment. This is *normal.*" He drew on his cigar. "But more important for Balam . . . very soon before he came to me, he was with friends in Antigua. Maybe they are sixteen, seventeen years old. You know the Parque Central in Antigua? The fountain?"

I nodded.

"They climb on top of the fountain. Children, you understand, playing, *verdad*? The police come, they take the children off the fountain, the children begin to fight back, they are punching the police, hitting them. The police place Balam and his friends in the jail. They beat Balam, many times. He will not tell them his name, so they keep him in the jail, with no toilet and no food, for three, maybe four days. Balam will not tell them his name. Finally, he is let go. And after that, Balam does not want to go to school. He does not want to go back to Canada. He does not want a job. He wants only to kill. *Entiendes*? This is how one makes a revolutionary. Balam would have been an asset in my time. But now, the civil war is ending. Balam does not want to be a guerilla. He is angry, but no one has taught him how to channel his anger. He does not believe in a cause."

He took a long puff from his cigar and tapped the ash. With his free hand, he laid an index finger across his lip, talking through it, pulling the finger away to punctuate his words. "And this is how Balam came to me. I taught him to focus his anger. I taught him how to be a man. I taught him how to make a very good living, to see the world and to—I do not know this word in English—to *aprovechar*, everything that this world has to offer. To take the good and the bad. And I tell you, for two years Balam does very good work for me. He is like a ghost, *verdad*? He is gone. No one sees him and lives to speak of him. He is very good." The Old Man gave me a serious, studied look. His eyes were piercing, drilling into me, as if pondering the answer to a question I had not dared to pose.

"Yes . . . there was a problem. He is psychotic, no? He likes the killing—too much. In my day, it was something that we had to do. But Balam . . . he chose this path. His family, they are not poor. His father is still in Canada—he could return, have another life. His mother lives a quiet life in the highlands. The rest of his family is in the capital, very successful, many businesses. This is a young man with many choices. But he likes to kill, very much. And this," he waved his hand in the air, "this is not good. All of this, all this business. To go to *el Norte* and kill so many people, so many who are no threat to us. So many unnecessary killings, this is not what I come from. And to kill an agent of the CIA—this is very, very stupid. You and I can agree on this, I am certain."

He looked to me for a response. I nodded again.

"And to try to kill a woman? Because she rejected him? *Una vergüenza.* And the girl Ashley? I worked too hard to protect her to have her thrown away like this."

The name was like a bullet, a hollow-point. "You protected Ashley? I don't understand."

He took a deep breath. "El Canche." He thumped the table with a closed fist, just loud enough. "You call him McCaffrey. We call him El Canche, the blond. You know the Deh Eme Effe, of course."

It took me a second. He slurred it together, *DehEmeEffe* —DMF. The Death Master File. It sounded even more sinister in Spanish. "*Claro.*"

"In the past, we used the DMF to remove the trace of

an asset. We have people in the Social Security. One . . . *golpe de teclado?*" He mimed tapping a keyboard.

"Keystroke."

"*Ahorita*, you are dead. It was useful. You get a new identity, you work for us, there is nothing of your old life. But now, in the modern day, with computers and credit cards, there is much fear of 'identity theft.' Too many people are looking. To be on the DMF—it is like an advertisement. Now, one of my associates has some ideas. Use the DMF for a target. Perhaps after a contract—bang, you are not, and *punto*, you never were. Or perhaps, because to be on the DMF is so upsetting when you yet live, it becomes a tool to disassemble the life of a target. *Punto*, you are dead on paper. *Entonces*, in the chaos—now you are dead, *en serio*."

He puffed on his cigar, turning it, getting the orange glow going. "It was only a discussion. Nothing decided, nothing—actionable." He punctuated his words with the cigar. "El Canche learns that we have this tool, this leverage. He is *una oportunista*—he doesn't think. As he found you—because his DAUGHTER died—" he squeezed his face in disgust, "he takes the first person who comes along. Ashley. He wants her help—someone already in trouble, someone disposable—and he has her added to the DMF. When I learned she was his family . . . I was furious. You do not do this. You do not expose your blood. It is like I told you, it is an advertisement, *verdad?* We also have enemies. He put her at great risk. THAT is why I insisted El Canche bring her in. Protect her. For her own safety. THAT is why I would not take her off of the DMF—that name cannot be hers ever again. THAT is why I had El Canche killed."

"That was you."

"Sí, pues. Balam was to kill him with his own gun, blame you. But we were forced to make other arrangements. I told El Canche two years ago I would kill him if anything happened to Ashley. The girl was an innocent." He pointed the cigar at me. "We agree, you and I. There is a way to live, and there are many ways not to live. My profession is unusual, yes, but my view of the world is no different from yours. One does not expose an innocent to misfortune without reason. One does not kill a woman. And even in my practice, one does not confuse the surgery of a tumor with the removal of the entire limb. So—" he put his cigar down and shifted in his seat so that we were directly eye to eye, "I think that you have come here for something, Mr. David Crane." He pronounced it Da-veed. "I think that you want something from me. And I am ready to listen. But you must be very careful what you ask of me. This is why I want you to know me, to know who I am, what we are. We are not El Pulpo. We are not the CIA. We are a small business that has survived many decades, and we will continue to survive. Not me," he laughed bombastically, truly amused, "I will be dead very soon. But I do not like heroes, Mr. Crane. I killed too many in my youth. Heroes are always a—what is the word—a disappointment. You cannot stop the world, my friend. You cannot stop history, verdad? And the future—it is as I said. There is no future. Now," he smiled benignly, "what can I do for you?"

I cleared my throat and took a long pull off my now-tepid Coke. "I want Balam."

"Mmmm . . ." He tilted his head and looked at me,

sizing me up. "Of course. You love the girl very much, *verdad*?"

"I do. I came for her."

"You understand, we have no interest in the girl. What is done is done. And you, also, David Crane. You were of great use to us, but no longer. You cannot help us while alive, but . . ." he shrugged his bushy eyebrows, "you are also no use to us dead. In this way, both you and your woman are safe."

"Thank you." I didn't know what else to say.

"But it is interesting to me, my friend. You have come here for love." He reached out and slapped me on the shoulder and began to laugh again. "Very stupid, no? You come to this place, to a strange country. Your friends, your police cannot help you—you don't know if I will kill you. You come to my city, where I own the police, you come to my home, knowing that I know you." He was laughing with full force now and spoke through it. "And you come to me? For love?" He laughed for a long time and fell into a coughing fit, a choking rattle that left him gasping.

The señora appeared with a glass of water and slapped him on the back until he regained control.

He sipped at the water, blinked a tear from his eye, and sent the woman away. He looked at me with a sudden fierceness. "You want to kill him." It wasn't a question.

I blinked. "I want to take him back alive."

"That, I cannot allow. Even if I wanted to, *entiendes?* Balam knows very much about our organization. If you were able to capture him, you would never leave this country alive. No one would consult me for a decision.

Because you see—*ahorita*, I am primarily a consultant. Every day, decisions are made beneath me. And that is beneath me. They will not know you. They know only that this is Balam, in handcuffs, with a gringo who is not the CIA and—bang! Bang!" He pounded the table and my heart palpitated. "The FBI is looking for him also, *verdad?* And the CIA."

"But they haven't found him."

He worked his eyebrows. "In this moment, we are helping him still. He is in the capital. He waits."

"Waits for what?"

"He waits for me. To tell him what he will do next. He knows he has made me unhappy, *verdad?* Now I must begin again. Our operation in California is finished. Almost everyone is dead. The survivors are wounded, deported. Do you know what trouble you and your woman have caused? What trouble Balam has caused? You—I understand. You must fight for your life, and you must fight for your love. But Balam was my apprentice—like a son to me. And this . . ." He wrinkled up his face in disgust. "He has become a liability. And I cannot let the FBI have him alive. And I would prefer the CIA not have him at all. They will kill him, yes, but they will torture him first. He is still my blood. I do not want him to suffer."

I had no idea what to say. I just sat there, drinking my Coke like a twelve-year-old boy enduring the ramblings of his grandfather. The Old Man grabbed his cigar from the ashtray and stood up, pushing his chair back and making it squeak on the stone floor. He tapped the tabletop.

"*Bien*. It is decided. You will go to Lago de Atitlán, in the highlands. You will wait. It is nice there, you will like it. Find a quiet place and wait. Someone will contact you when Balam will come, and where. Do you have a weapon?"

I must have flinched. *After now, there is nothing.* As the Old Man's portentous *now* fell across me, my lack of a future like a cold draft, I must have flinched. The Old Man leaned in, his ham-hock fists on the table, eyes boring into mine.

"What did you think, David? I would leave you alive for no reason? Out of the goodness of my heart?" He smiled, and it reminded me there were crocodiles in this corner of the world. He gestured in the direction the señora had gone. "I might give you to María, let her keep you in the kitchen and feed you to the dogs—little by little. You don't know her past." He looked suddenly younger. "Or do it with my bare hands, just to feel the blood in my heart again." I held his gaze, but it wasn't easy. "You are alive but for the grace of me," he said, thumping his chest, "and grace is never free."

I found my voice: "No. I don't have a weapon."

"We will provide you with a weapon. And when it is done, I have someone in Sololá who will deliver his body to the FBI. I don't want to see him again, alive or dead." He straightened up and turned away, ophidian, finished.

"How will you find me?"

He looked back over his shoulder without making eye contact. "Balam can hide in this country. Maybe he can disappear. But not you, gringo. I will always know where you are. Do this for me and I will no longer notice. *Buena suerte.*"

I had been assigned the task of assassinating the assassin Balam.

* * *

The next morning I took the bus back to Guatemala City and ignored the passing countryside, just staring at the TV showing *The Princess Bride* dubbed in Spanish. Twice. The humor of the priest's speech impediment—*mawwiage, twue wuv*—was completely lost. When I arrived in the capital I walked a few blocks to a wide, dirt plaza that served as the way station for chicken buses to Antigua. The buses were used school buses from the States, yellow Blue Bird buses repainted in bright reds, blues, and greens, with garish detailing. I boarded one, and as we made our way through the city the *ayudante* shoved his way through the bus collecting fares.

The highway took us up out of the smog-filled bowl of Guatemala City, leading us rapidly away. In under an hour we came to the turn-off to Antigua, the scenery already green and lush, and I got off with a few other stragglers and waited by the roadside until another bus pulled over, the *ayudante* leaning out of the still-moving bus to shout, "Panajachel!"

We stopped at the crossroads wasteland of Chimaltenango, a dusty, chaotic smattering of faded clapboards and diesel fumes. People got on; people got off. A few young men wore blue jeans and baseball caps, but most of the passengers were indigenous women, dark-skinned, carrying large bundles and children, and dressed in the manner they'd had for centuries, ankle-length woven skirts and embroidered *huípiles*. Vendors came in through the back door and worked their way to the front, barking, selling bottled water, chips, homemade snacks in blanket-covered baskets. The bus was crowded now, and the passengers wedged into the benches—designed for two—in threes. I found myself snuggled up between a young man, pulling his cap down low and reading *El Diario*—or, at least, staring at the bikini-clad woman featured like a PG version of *The Sun*'s page three—and an indigenous woman. She had only one ass cheek on the bench, her weight supported by the woman with one cheek on the adjacent bench.

We wound through majestic hills, climbing steadily upward, the countryside increasingly and impressively verdant. We turned off at another crossroads, the nascent town of Los Encuentros. I jumped off the bus to take a piss behind a line of shacks. Vending carts were lined up like hot dog stands but with portable fryers behind glass. I bought some french fries, given to me in a brown paper bag with ketchup and salsa verde dumped over the top. They were magnificent.

I stood as we wound our way down from the crest of the hill, peeking out the windows to watch field workers harvesting potatoes. As we pulled in to the local capital, Sololá, traffic came to a standstill. It was market day, and as we shuddered to a stop next to the main square and the bus emptied out, I blinked at the cornucopia of color in the market, the brightly painted chicken buses, the rows of stunning vegetables, the fabric and handicrafts for sale, bright yellow chicks chirping in netted baskets, the hordes of Mayans in multicolored handmade clothing. The men wore straw cowboy hats, breechcloths over pajama-like woven pants, and long-sleeved shirts that were more like jackets, rococo in their decoration, almost Las Vegas in bright pinks and gold, some with resplendent birds stitched on the back.

My empty bus filled with new passengers, and vendors passed *helados* up through the open windows. I was now not just the only gringo, but the only passenger not wearing indigenous dress. I watched with amazement as a woman with two kids, forced to stand, handed off the smaller child to a stranger across the crowded bus. None of the children on board cried or whimpered, they simply stared out at the world through wide, opalescent eyes.

The road was steep and winding, crawling steadily downward, and I caught fleeting, dreamlike glimpses of the lake in its splendor, a sea of blue, towered over authoritatively by the volcanoes Atitlán and Tolimán. In the final stretch of road above Lago de Atitlán the view opened up completely, and I took in the overpowering beauty of the lake, mesmerized by its size and clarity. San Pedro, the volcano at the far end, loomed domineering and yet distant, the lake supine, rippled, reflecting the clouds in impressionistic shards, the town of Panajachel a human joke in the face of natural accomplishment.

I thought of the Old Man, and quietly thanked him for sending me to such a beautiful place.

Panajachel was a tourist trap, with too many smiling gringos for my taste. English and German crackled in the air in restaurants and cafés, and I couldn't get through a meal without being asked to buy something by a ridiculously cute—yet infinitely annoying—young Mayan girl. I couldn't imagine how the Old Man's people could find me in such a place, so speckled with white faces, but I believed him, and I remembered his recommendation to *find a quiet place.* It was good advice for one preparing to become a killer.

On my second day at the lake I went to the public dock, got on a *lancha*—a small speed boat—and asked the *capitán* to take me somewhere quiet. The *lancha* was crowded, and at each stop I helped *abuelitas* with their innumerable packages. Villages dotted the coastline of the lake, small roads and clusters of domiciles climbing up into the hills. It was the rainy season, the *capitán* told me, and the lake was high, the hillsides green. The *lancha* pulled in amongst reeds and floating bits of volcanic rock, and I got out and, for a couple of quetzales, allowed a small boy to lead me to a hotel. It was a small room, a small hotel, a small village.

I had no idea where I was. I didn't care. There were gringos living amongst the indigenous—shaggy, unkempt hippies in Guatemalan clothing who said little more than *hola* to me. The tourists, passing through for a day or two of relaxation, were either European or Israeli and didn't speak to me at all. The local population spoke a Mayan dialect, either Cakchiquel or Tz'utujil, I assumed, and their Spanish wasn't any better than mine. There was little reason to talk to anyone. I settled in easily into the hotel that was little more than a string of tiny A-frame bungalows, went for morning swims in the lake, breathless in the cool clarity of the water; bought fresh vegetables from women squatting at the side of a road too narrow to be called a road; found a *comedor* that served hot meals, a *chuleta*, or stringy chicken, with pitch-black beans more flavorful than beef; sat out at night staring at the lake in the moonlight, smoking Rubios and sipping at a bottle of Old Friend I'd brought from Pana.

Three days later there was a knock on my bungalow door. I didn't have to wonder. A nondescript Guatemalan man, young enough to be a college student, handed me a small backpack. I opened it up: a Smith & Wesson .38 Special and a box of shells.

"There may not be a position for a rifle," he said, by way of explanation. "El Viejo told me you would be more comfortable with this."

"It's fine," I said. "Where?"

"In two days he will be in Santa Cruz. At four o'clock, *más o menos*, he will come by *lancha* from Pana, and go to the café at la Iguana Perdida. He is coming for a job, but the job is not there. Understand?"

"I understand." They were baiting him, making my life easier.

"*Adios.*" He was gone. He didn't say, *Hasta luego*; he had no intention of seeing me again.

I spent the next two days resting, smoking, and thinking, with long walks up into the hills to practice on Coke bottles, getting the feel of someone else's gun.

The day was beaming with intensity, the sun shining down in all its glorious alacrity. I wanted to be unseen, so decided not to take the *lancha*. I started off on the road a little before one o'clock, climbing over the first crest to look back at Volcán San Pedro keeping vigil from across the lake. I turned my back on it, wondering if I would ever see it again. The sides of the road were cluttered with tiny yellow butterflies. They knew nothing.

I passed a few men working on a wall, and a number of women in *huípiles* carrying baskets on their heads. Every now and then I had to step to the side to make way for a *camioneta*, a pickup truck packed with passengers clutching the steel rails on the sides of the bed—an informal mode of public transportation.

At a tiny village the proper road petered out over a pedestrian bridge and I continued on a rough path that snaked past thatched houses, meandering through the foliage. I pushed on to the first big hill, and at the top of it my shirt was already wet with sweat, my smoker's lungs gasping for breath. The path clung to the sides of the hills, moving along through coffee plants, the sun blazing.

After an hour and a half of heavy puffing, pushing myself up and down the sinewy path, I hit another village. The path had branched off a number of times, and I realized that I must have taken a wrong turn. I was near the water's edge, at a stone pathway that led to hundreds of stone steps, the entryway to an expensive hotel. I walked up them, panting, bypassing the hotel, finally reaching the road that, I hoped, would lead me to the next village—Santa Cruz.

The thunder was rolling in the distance, and I could see menacing black clouds and their gray message raining down over the far side of the lake. The afternoon rains had begun early, and the opposite shore was now completely invisible. San Pedro had disappeared, as had the tops of the volcanoes Tolimán and Atitlán.

I had a good forty-five minutes to go, and doubted I'd beat the storm. It didn't matter. My gun was tied up well in a plastic bag in my satchel. I put on my cheap rain jacket and pushed on.

Within twenty minutes the storm broke over my head. The thunder was deafening, ravishing, making the coffee plants shudder. The rain came down in large, cold bullets, pelting me and making percussive music on the surrounding foliage. My pants were immediately soaked through from rubbing up against the vegetation lining the path. Five more minutes and my cheap rain jacket was a clinging plastic sieve. The dirt path beneath my feet turned into a river. Every inch of me was drenched to the bone, and only pushing on kept me from freezing.

I heard a squishing and a *"Buenas tardes,"* and a local ran past me with a piece of plastic sheeting drawn across him like a cape. A few minutes later, as I tried to straddle the stream running under me, I saw the man ahead, pulled over and waiting for me. He told me in Spanish that the path ahead was nothing but a waterfall.

"A dónde vas?" he asked.

"Santa Cruz."

"Vámonos en el campo." He led the way off the path, and we stumbled over gnarled roots, tripping over errant bits of barbed wire before coming into a soccer field that had become a marsh. We trudged through, and in a few minutes we were on a paved road and he was bidding me farewell, the pueblo of Santa Cruz before me.

I followed the road up, fairly certain that I was going the wrong way. It was almost four; he would be arriving from Pana any minute. I felt like an idiot for walking. My best chance would be to catch him at the docks before he entered la Iguana Perdida, but I needed to get my wits about me.

I stopped at a little *tienda*, a tiny shack with an open window, operated by two little girls, probably sisters, maybe eleven and nine years old. I asked for a bottle of water and picked up a package of Chikys, apologizing profusely for the fact that I only had a hundred-quetzal note on me. The younger girl, with a radiant smile and a brilliantly colored *huipil*, ran off to fetch change, so I leaned against the window ledge and took a long pull of water. The chocolate cookies were delicious and had the crisp taste of a last meal. The rain had slacked off into a sporadic drizzle. The girl came back with my change, giggling as she dodged raindrops, followed by a woman who was laughing hysterically at the state of her umbrella. The fabric had slipped off the ends of the spokes, and it looked like she was holding the dried, molted exoskeleton of an oversized spider. The older girl helped her stretch it back out and the woman went off into the rain.

I was about to leave when a local authority came over with a gun in a holster at his side. I twitched a moment, relaxing when I realized that, to him, I was just another wet gringo. He bought a plastic bottle of Pepsi and disappeared around the corner of the *tienda*.

I pulled off my drenched rain jacket and tried to squeeze some of the water out of my shirt. The Xocomil was blowing—the afternoon southeasterly wind that chops the lake with whitecaps—and I was starting to shiver. It was time.

I stepped around the corner of the *tienda* and looked down the stone path, made of small rocks patched together to form a rough, semipaved pathway that wound down the hill to the docks like a miniature Lombard Street. It was a long, steep climb down to the water. I was stuffing my jacket into my satchel, keeping an eye on the path, when I caught a strange tingling sensation. There was a young man coming up the hill toward me, dressed in jeans, a plaid shirt, and a simple canvas jacket; an ordinary-looking Guatemalan. If it hadn't been for the sick feeling in my stomach I might not have recognized him.

It was Sharkskin. Balam. The brow and the air of menace about him was unmistakable. I ducked back behind the *tienda* and peeked out. He hadn't seen me; he was walking with his head slightly down, his hair damp from the rain, watching his step on the path. I couldn't wonder about why he had come up into town; it didn't matter. I went around to the end of the *tienda* and stepped off the road onto the muddy embankment. I half-slid down the side wall, coming to the back of the *tienda* and fumbling in my satchel. I could see him approaching through the brush, and got my hand inside the plastic bag, gripping the butt of the gun, sneaking toward the corner of the *tienda* as he passed by, mere feet away from me. It had to be now. He wouldn't hesitate; I couldn't either.

I dropped my satchel in the mud, my hand coming out with the gun, still covered by the ridiculous blue plastic bag. The weapon was dry but my hands were slick. I clicked the safety off. I stepped up out of the slop and onto the stone path, raising the gun and drawing a bead on him, when one of the stones lining the edge of the path broke away. My feet went out from under me and I slipped into the mud. Balam stopped and turned. In a flash of recognition he reached into his jacket and came out with a pistol, moving quickly toward me, flashing that familiar grin.

"*Oye!*"

We both flinched. The local cop was coming up the

path below us, the half-empty Pepsi bottle in his hand. He dropped the bottle and reached for his gun but never got it out of the holster. Balam turned and fired off a shot, aiming too low, hitting the cop somewhere below the waist and putting him down with a bloodcurdling cry, and the little girls in the *tienda* screamed. The Pepsi bottle bounced down the hill in slow motion, clattering on the stones.

I raised my bag-wrapped gun from a crouch and squeezed on the inhale, putting one neatly into the front of Balam's shoulder as he pivoted to aim at me. The impact pushed his shoulder back and spun him halfway around, but I'd hit the wrong shoulder—the gun was in his other hand, and he didn't drop it. I managed to scramble to my feet as he spun back at me in a frantic, twitching gesture, raising his gun toward me again, the grin still in place. I put one in his chest, and the grin was just starting to fade when I made it disappear completely with another shot to the throat.

I walked toward him, holding a shredded blue plastic bag. I kicked the gun out of his hand—it was McCaffrey's goddamned Baby Glock—and it skittered along the cobblestones and stopped in the gutter. He was twitching and gurgling; you couldn't call it breathing.

He looked up at me, not with hatred in his eyes, but with something akin to sadness.

"For Susan," I said. "And for Ash."

Men had come out into the street and were standing around nervously watching the dead man on the road, as women looked on from doorways, holding their children close. I pulled my satchel out of the mud and walked over to the local cop, lying back in the arms of an older man. He had been hit in the leg; his face was cramped in pain, but he wasn't losing too much blood. He would live. He would have a great story to tell his grandkids. He looked up at me.

"*Gracias.*"

"*De nada.*"

I walked away. The street went from a simmer to a rolling boil, men and women running to the cop to tend to his wounds, others hurrying to throw a blanket over the dead man and get him out of the street. A crowd was forming and I felt strangely invisible as I slipped down the path, winding my way along the slippery stone walk, taking the slow bends, approaching the dock. An off-duty *lancha capitán* told me that the next boat would be there in ten minutes, so I went into the café and ordered a coffee. I was reaching for my money when I realized that I still had the blue bag—and the gun—in my hand. I put it away, took my coffee to the terrace, and made faces at a three-year-old English girl sitting with her parents, bored. We waited for the boat together, and the rain picked up again with a sudden fury that pelted the dock and made us pull our chairs back farther on the terrace. Then it stopped.

I've adopted a rhythm without even trying. I rented a small house up the hill from the lake, just a couple rooms with a flush toilet and a gas stove and electricity. Most of my days are spent idly, at the lake, swimming, lying on the rocks, lizard-like, waiting to dry, getting too hot, jumping back in. In the afternoons, before the rains come, I do a little shopping, walking slowly, hearing the *clip clop* of my sandals on the stone path and the swish of my mesh bag slung over one shoulder. There are always birds chirping in the trees, strange, alien birdsongs, and on the rocks, near the lake, the sporadic skitter of lizards. And the dogs—a lot of dogs, what the locals call *chuchos*, near-feral, wandering free, entrenched in the endless pursuit of food and the infinite allure of a bitch in heat. At night, when the village is completely dark and the lake luminescent in the starlight, the dogs bark endlessly, staking territory, fighting and snarling at each other, occasionally barking in ones and twos just to hear themselves speak, listening to their voices echo off the hills surrounding the lake. Sometimes lightning flashes behind the volcanoes, the thunder too far away to hear, the silhouette of the volcanoes starkly visible for a moment, then fading back into obscurity.

I cook breakfast, usually just eggs scrambled with fresh peppers, onions, and tomatoes, and beans, the refried black beans that are so special here, and sometimes fresh cheese made locally, and fresh tortillas that I get from a man on the path. I smoke the local cigarettes. I buy fruits and vegetables from indigenous women, enraptured by their freshness and lack of pesticides, mangoes and papayas and pineapples, several different kinds of bananas, tomatoes as sweet as plums, bell peppers as crisp as corn chips. I pick out strange new items to sample: *pitaya, güisquil.*

When I swim, I swim toward the volcano, breaststroke, eyes open both below and above the water, and as I surface I feel almost amphibious, staring at the volcano—ageless, older than man—and dream in my waking life of a time when jaguars roamed the highlands and monkeys still lurked in the trees. It wasn't that long ago, I am told. I feel as if I have fallen backward in time.

A week here is like a lifetime in the States. Only a week since the man appeared at my door again and told me that Balam's body was shipped to the States, only a week since I sent word to Chinatown. A week here can change your mind about everything—about life, about the reason for it, about why yours turned out the way it did. I see it all around me—gringos who came for a weekend and stayed two years, travelers who were on vacation and decided to quit their jobs, loners who met someone and changed the entire trajectory of their lives. Anything is possible in a place such as this. And like all extremes, the opposite is equally true—nothing is possible in a place such as this.

I've been dreaming. Sleeping without alcohol has opened my unconscious, and my dreams have overtaken me, inoculated me. Always, I am dreaming of her. Of a love that could drive a man to kill another. I am dreaming of a woman I barely know, a woman so beautiful that I shiver at the thought of her, at the memory of her touch.

I am waiting for her. When she arrives, I will be here. Waiting.

Acknowledgments

This book was born in South San Francisco, raised on Lake Atitlán in Guatemala, and revised and edited in Brooklyn and New Orleans. Thanks to my associates and accomplices in all of the above, particularly:

Thanks to my father, Duane Spinelli, for letting me slide on the rent on his childhood home in SSF for a couple of months while I was first imagining Ashley. This book owes so much to that house. Thanks to my Uncle Steve, my cousins (the Wrecking Crew), Patricia Dixon (RIP), and my grandparents, Burnell and Margaret (RIP), for making that time so memorable. Thanks, Mom, for always taking us to California.

Tremendous thanks to *mi hermano* Balam Sapper for letting me steal so liberally from his life, and for all the feedback and suggestions. Thanks to everyone at the lake who supported and distracted me during my working sabbaticals. Raising a glass to Nikki Lane, Eva Zeppa, and all the *chuchos*. This book owes much to that place too.

Thanks to Robert Lee for encouraging me to finish the book once I figured out where it was going, and for design counsel; to Will Kenton for always being both supportive and critical; and thanks always to Mike DeCapite for encouragement and off-line advice beyond odds. Thanks to Meghan Carey Kates for bringing it home once again with the stunning cover design. Thanks also to Kimberlee Hewitt for help with photo retouching, and to Elizabeth Fox Poff for all the work on 13spinelli.com.

Thanks to Daniel Maurer for taking an interest in me and putting me on the *Bedford + Bowery* team.

THANK YOU, Aaron Petrovich, for taking a chance on a book by a random guy at BookExpo America, for loving it, nurturing it, and demanding it be better than it was. Thanks to Johnny Temple for publishing it, and to Ibrahim Ahmad, Johanna Ingalls, Susannah Lawrence, and everyone at Akashic for all the hard work.

Most of all, thanks to my wife, Ronit Schlam, for her efforts as publicist and editor, and for encouraging me to keep putting myself out there. I wouldn't have made it this far otherwise. I hope you enjoy this book (the one the moms can read).

Grateful acknowledgment to *Bitter Fruit* by Stephen Schlesinger and Stephen Kinzer, which is recommended reading for anyone interested in the atrocities in Guatemala perpetrated by the United States in the 1950s.

Additional acknowledgment to *SFGate* for details on unsolved murders in the Bay Area:

Zamora, Jim Herron. "S.F. on Grim Pace to Set Homicide Mark in '96." February 7, 1996.

Sward, Susan. "SLAYING UNSOLVED/Cops Explore Connections, Coincidences in Natali Death." June 4, 1997.

"EAST BAY/Oakland Man Slain—Parked in Own Driveway." August 19, 1997.

And to the *New York Times* for the Michael DeVine story:

Dillon, Sam. "On Her Guatemalan Ranch, American Retraces Slaying." March 28, 1995.

Dillon, Sam. "Guatemalan Chief Tells Colonel to Sue." March 30, 1995.

Ronit Schlam

BRADLEY SPINELLI is the author of the novel *Killing Williamsburg*, and the writer/director of the film *#AnnieHall*, which the *Village Voice* called "fascinating." He contributes to *Bedford + Bowery* and lives in Brooklyn.